THE INDIGO HOURS

Maria Sledmere is a poet, editor and scholar living in Glasgow. Her most recent publications are *Languishing, cute* — with Ian Macartney (Tapsalteerie, 2025), *Midsummer Song* (Tenement Press, 2024) and *Cinders* (Krupskaya, 2024). She is senior lecturer in English & Creative Writing at the University of Strathclyde, managing editor of SPAM Press and one half of the performance duo Project Somnolence.

Also by Maria Sledmere

the weird folds: everyday poems from the anthropocene [editor, with Rhian Williams]
(Dostoyevsky Wannabe, 2020)

The Luna Erratum (Dostoyevsky Wannabe, 2021)

Sonnets for Hooch [with Mau Baiocco and Luce Lovell] (Fathomsun, 2021)

String Feeling (Erotoplasty Editions, 2022)

Visions & Feed (HVTN Press, 2022)

The Last Song: Words for Frightened Rabbit [editor, with Aaron Kent]
(Broken Sleep Books, 2023)

Cocoa and Nothing [with Colin Herd] (SPAM Press, 2023)

An Aura of Plasma Around the Sun (Hem Press, 2023)

Cinders (Krupskaya, 2024)

Midsummer Song (Hypercritique) (Tenement Press, 2024)

Languishing, cute [with Ian Macartney] (Tapsalteerie, 2025)

ISBN: 978-1-917617-41-3

Cover designed by Aaron Kent

Cover image: © gizemg / Adobe Stock

Edited by Alice Booker

Typeset by Aaron Kent

Broken Sleep Books Ltd
PO BOX 102
Llandysul
SA44 9BG

The Indigo Hours

Maria Sledmere

Broken Sleep Books

...You said nothing was worth pursuing, in the end, if it wasn't a case of pleasure. Or did I say that. I said something about growing older. Our conversation looped in ribbons – three shades of green – then stilled around a void. We'd soon enough stop speaking. We were a starlight sugar level. What was in that case? Your mother nurtured white poppies so that every May when the garden darkened all you could see were their pale wee faces, hardening against the dark like eyes. The many-eyed garden of your mother. A space we locked away. I remember kissing you then, close to the edge. The way you tasted milky. That was a pleasure way. How I wanted this bottled. Closer to lilac in the light. Your eyes strained from screens I was kissing you better, kissing them close to sleep. Of course, we hid from your mother, and pretty much everyone else, when we kissed. You poured a glass of milk from the fridge.

There was pleasure, something of the Romantics I read at school: this Wordsworthian thing about pleasure. No one around me could tolerate this level of daffodil crap. As it was, I was hoarding Dorothy's journals and obsessing over her drinking tea, with such constancy it put my old scrolling habits to shame. Break for tea, tea at breakfast. Spill the tea. I've been trying, casually, to make statements of correlation between tea consumption and weather. There was pleasure there. My blood all rich with caffeine, twirling on a spot to make motion of the light in your eyes and speech at the party. Green light tea. It's all gossip. What? Other people speak of the narrative lapse of cigarettes. Okay so it's raining. I'm scrolling. You're typing. There was a rhythm to our quitting, arrangements of sugary negative space. With words we drew a new foreground…

…When all we wanted in the end was to disappear (in one another). The rain became mist, then milky distance. For drawing one sigh is the sound of the other, whose motion you can hardly class as light. At work, when they talked about it, teased us, all I could think of was your breath. I conducted desire in unruly shifts. There could be no fresh release. Was it me, no, would I ever?

"Who *was it* Marlene?"

Mostly I drifted towards the one table where a window let in the afternoon, the sheer fact of its atmosphere. I brought over rusted pots of Twinings Breakfast tea, my fingers dusty from arranging the tablet just so on the side. Hospitality is the trading of one thing for the other, a ceaseless admittance of instability. Here you go. Speech acts for self-erasure. Melt in your mouth.

Nobody knows what they really want. Why think five years or even a meal ahead?

I was not always in this line of business; or as a matter of fact in this, the other.

Your mother, like others, would never know enough to ask what I did.

Shift patterns promote idleness. I fall into one loophole only to catch breath on the start of the next, till the hours slack a lariat of absence around my nervous system. So even as I pace, carrying plates, I say it again I miss you. There's a beat.

Whose? Here I am, still picking at blood flakes in the palm of my hand.

A chef picking chilli flakes from Tesco.

Sometimes, I'm like Emily. It's like Hi, I'm no one! When I write this, who are you?

I had a friend called Emily
and we were so young: we fell
into our respective wardrobes.

What age are we to receive first self-assurances, like appreciate life's big thrust, blood in our veins and everything? When very sapling, a babe on the floor must be approximate; just as gold might be an unseen sun, but it's just the glint of a pound, someone's earring. Lying on the carpet like that, upside down, is really an athletic feat. Pretend you are looking for something, when all this adds up to a defiance of gravity. I collect the words *kidney, alias, shelf, artichoke* & *stones*.

*
**

I don't remember that much from my first day at school. I was intrigued by all the sudden haircuts, styles abounding, strange imitations of pop stars from telly. Nobody had a *haircut* before my first day at school. We didn't watch that kind of television at home. We looked at magazines in the dentist's office. Mum cut our fringes with zig zag scissors because she loved David Bowie. It was the nineties and every boy was a boy in a boy band, at the very least virtually, at the very least as miniatures — those plastic statuettes! Girls with plaits, whose process of elaborate fashioning I'd contemplate like sculptural algebra. I remember mostly the first hour of class, sitting round a table presided over by this kid, a boy shorter than me but with god's own aura about him. Even at five, his face looked wrinkled, as if his birth was the great difficulty of his life from which he would never recover. He kept saying "Aye aye aye aye aye" over and over. I didn't know what Aye meant. I felt glitchy and English. I hated to feel English, but it seemed I'd feel glitchy for the rest of my existence, like somebody forgot to finish my code, so I would never land at Subject. The Aye seemed to emanate power around him. I thought he was saying "I I I I I" and each "I" was like another candle liberally stabbed into the invisible cake he had in front of him, the icing mushing everywhere. Happy birthday to the brand new day. I didn't get it. I mean obviously he was saying yes to something. But in that moment I just thought he was asserting himself, his I-ness, aye sure, over and over. I didn't know you could just take from the room and add a fat chunk of you like that. Someone kicking me hard in the shins. Cherry red mark and shining. A candle to kingdom come.

Spring came and I could hardly believe it. Blossomy blossomy realm of the possible. Each year I wrote something to that effect in my diary. Which is like saying, okay fine you can sleep after all. The time I stupidly toasted a sheet of fluoxetine, and the blister pack crinkled amber-brown, inedible.

In The Meadows: people with beauty's aggression, shaking the trees for their 'Instagram blossom.'

A bad cartwheel breaking a leg.

Yes yes yes yes yes. It was like saying etcetera. For years, I made wishes on ayes. Clung petals.

Say yes.

*
**

How happy I was to see forget-me-nots. I picked a bench parallel with another bench, upon which an old man sat staring at nothing. Old men around here do this a lot. They indulge in the montage of the past. I have watched them do it as bus stops, crossroads, lay-bys. Mostly they do it in bars. I wonder if you snapped your fingers in their face, would they, as it were, snap out of it? I wonder if they dream in sepia. It occurred to me that I wanted to smile at him. I hoped he watched me as I photographed the little blue flowers, so we could share that simple pleasure of return. The flowers came back, despite everything. Emerged from the snow whose ceaseless fall was named beastly. I wanted to gather them up in bunches, but instead I left them, easy as breezes.

My old man is a vanishing man.

See how he really sees everything.

*
**

Feels perverse but it wasn't even dark and I was on YouTube, listening to 'You Missed My Heart' over and over, something shivering in my ribs. The singer's face wasn't perfectly symmetrical, but it seemed carved from the quartz of MTV. She had silver hair and I hardly remembered her from reality, mostly the shimmer of her voice and my nervousness. It was summer, cloying and hot and really I was desperate to drink over anything. Now a blanket around me.

Now every building familiar.

I was drunk.

I was drunk at beautiful school.

I had a little breath, inflamed with Bell's.

This was the cheapest, strongest option on the Wetherspoons menu.

What did you do?

Education hit upon plot holes. There were things even teachers couldn't give me straight answers to, like whether you should put a dash in 'no-one.'

Is that why old men do word games in papers? I sense they are looking for an error within language. An infrastructure of the urban replaced by crosswords. Something the journalist had unconsciously forgotten and the linguist incapable. If they could only source that accident, they'd prolong their lives, cheating the axial logic.

*
**

You said they'd all bailed. All my friends had bailed on me too, but there was no meeting between. I realised the common language had an expiry. So it was just us. A word like a need.

My exhaustion countered a fact. It was difficult, trying to pass on your ticket. Nobody wanted to venture out on a Sunday, but the park was packed, coming back strong from its sad hibernation.

I tried not to call them firework tulips. The imbalance of blood and chemicals. Upright and pluckable.

My legs burned and I burned thinking of how many places there are called Nowhere.

I would sleep for miles and miles.

Nowhere Lake, Nowhere Canyon, Nowhere Valley, Nowhere Coffee, Nowhere Salon, Nowhere Nowhere.

Where is where.

A chic location for relaxed endeavours.

Stamina an artefact of transient passions. I have tried in the dark not to miss you. Mist affected my screen to listlessness beneath the sheets.

My gin grows warm in its plastic bottle. I do not drink it. With my straw, I worry the slices of apple that bob to the surface. I feel guilty about the plastic and again go plastic at the backs of my knees. It's within me, I fear, mucilaginous object forgotten. A spoonful of brain. Molten into alcohol. Love Afterlife.

The park was still hoaching, and the police came because crowds of teens were pushing each other down the hill, swilling cider cans they tossed on the grass. The police wore high-vis grimaces and frog-marched the teenagers out of the park. I swear this never happens so totally. They made spaghetti of their arms in protest. The air was rich with the testosterone of rotting fruit. Days later, I discovered there was a stabbing. To the teens I said<>I will grow old like you. I will pick up your trash forever.

She played in this sweaty basement but of course that day I had not eaten since nine and my pulse was running high on what you might call twenty. Other people would go out to smoke in this scenario, but I stood there, floundering, focusing on the music. I wished I was twenty again. My blood was too shivery for nicotine. Everyone was there for the folk tunes but she made it a rock show, silvery in her baggy hoodie. I suppose I was watching for how wide her lips could go, swallowing vowels into songs like a kind of bright light swallowing flies in a porno. Everyone around me was so quiet it was like we were ill. Where would I be at twenty again, however many miles per hour? I gripped the sticky bar to stay steady.

The pool wasn't clean. It backed onto a warehouse, this sparkling exception of a summer garden. Who knew lindens could grow in Berlin. The lime leaves fell in the pool all through July and August. Nobody scooped them. I visited when the time was right / when I'd had enough. Liv kept cool glasses of lime and soda in the house for when I came in from the pool, which smelled of forest mulch among chlorine. I did clean sweeping strokes; I covered the pool back and forth. There was a time when I wasn't so precise. I'd do backstroke at the public pool back home; I'd swerve off my trajectory and whack some poor athlete in the head with my strokes. I learned a lot then. Learned to close my world, slim the lines, narrow and harden. Wrapped in a towel, aged twelve, I shivered on the patio as my grandmother told me I had 'childbearing hips.' Ever since then, I've carried any weight lopsided. The restaurant required me to lift chairs and tables, crates of glasses and sandwich board signs. I kept a bruise, permanently, on my left hipbone. At night I stroked the everchanging smudge of blue/purple/grey/green and wondered who it belonged to. The board signs flapped their truths in my fantasies, something about fresh deals, beauty sleep, are you ready.

I could try to describe the prairie. The cheddar-red homecoming sunsets, sense of the flame-tipped birches in early winter. The nowhereness of every mile lost. Honestly it was like a place from your dreams, *yours specifically*, a place in-between one world and the next. One girl and the next. Endless flatness. All hope of foliage had long been stamped into the ground, remaining but a texture on earth. People had disappeared on the prairie. Ruthie told me about the will-o'-the-wisp that lit little spirals in the air at night.

"If a story in which we escape a fire," she said. She didn't finish the conditional. She exhaled smoke. I tried to remember what fire we escaped, maybe a classroom in flames when the plug exploded. What teacher forgot to tell us to leave, spraying the flames herself. Blue fluid, red flame. Kicking open doors with her boots, toes of steel. On the prairie, your breath levelled out to a sigh. I could only watch it from my father's back garden, while the chickens squawked in their cage behind me. The thing about the prairie was you had to cross all that marshland to get there. You had to risk sinking.

So I would grow up there, on the prairie, developing my marshy alias.

Cam would paddle out in his father's canoe, idly streaming hardcore on his phone. I knew his whole history, kept cookies rehearsed below my tongue. When he got far enough, he didn't even bother with headphones, so the grunts and moans would mingle with the starlit buzz of mosquitos and crickets.

Even when he was a kid, he called me kid.

He said there were some kinds of pain you had to earn.

We'd skim stones on level water, one for every kiss we didn't give. I watched his peter out, twenty leaps later, behind the reeds.

These days, there's that empty feeling when I wake up, like when you drink too much tea before eating – except I don't – this watery attempt to fill up the absence stings and I feel nauseous just thinking about boiling the kettle.

"The will-o'-the-wisp will appear to you in the colour of your aura," Ruthie said. "Its trick is an unfinished business. You're best searching for it in early autumn, like an orgasm." She tried to convince me the wisp would lead to buried treasure. But it might just be the treasures of your mind, an unrealised epiphany. Some astrological bullshit ascribed to fairies. This was when Ruthie still wore all those beads, clicking up and down her wrists. She'd sign me up without asking to all these New Age mailing lists. Hayley hadn't left her yet. She was content; she thought she'd found the centre of the universe. She was a self-deprived dream kid. But that wisp would escape, would dance at the edge of her vision. She couldn't help but describe it to me, each time we sat at the back of my father's garden, trying to sort through all the precise and important things that had happened. It was her I first told about you. She looked at me once in a strange way, cocking her head just so. My nerves were on edge from the owls. The vowel sounds of owls. She said she'd seen my aura, faint as it was, finally. A cottony flicker in the night. She said it like a swear word.

Burning sky muscle before the bar shift.

The colour indigo is a sliver between one thing and the next: it's barely there.

I got my tarot read in this awkward restaurant where they sold illegal liqueurs at twentieth-century prices. The people around us ate plates of deep-fried delicacies, nested in beds of flattened seaweed, kimchi and salad, while I stared intently at the cards placed before me. Ruthie was so precise about these things. In-between each lay of the card, another greasy hair sweep. I said I was trying to reach for one purity in my life, that was the question I wanted to ask the cards. To retreat into a softness akin to the yolk of early reverie. There was a card where a red-hooded brownie protected her lay of colourful eggs; but all my cards were arboreal, spherical, cluttered with pentacles. It seemed I was tangled still in the roots of my past, treelines that stretched an eternity away from me. Darkness of presence. The Empress guards my unconscious. She has tresses of lush viridian hair, woven with roses. Is she trying to hide something? In the restaurant, sipping jasmine tea amid sweet spice, I thought about what I had done with you and it crisped around the edge of acceptance. The guilt lost a portion of its fat and grew lean, the fact of one thing and the next. So much I could tell but don't.

So much I'd reduce to cinders.

"I love you but I'm drunk" — our literal refrain. Sacred golden lager halo. We held each other while I went blurry and earnest. We walked out the club that night, over and over; the second time you threw your drink on the floor, it was wonderful. This sense of ourselves followed us home. The night another club burned down for real. I grew small in the boughs of your sprawling extroversion; then this reversed, and you did the shrinking, and I blinked for both of us. Ordered coffee because the words didn't work. We found these walls of glowing light to sleep inside. Our room. My tongue was also a luminescent tool.

The harmonies of that song about the Forth went I am, I am, I am, I am with a slight syncopation, release like a tidal pull and I thought a fucking book of us, I couldn't help it. No one knows.

The indigo light on the pool. In this house in Berlin that wasn't mine, I drank cold lime sodas on the porch, counting my blessings. Insert: reading the travel section of *Vogue* in airports, tasting paradise in glossy azure. More ice. I catch myself in these details, the taste of oysters described with cloying grossness, over-compensating. Bored at work, I tried to read that memoir of the chef, who describes his first oyster as sweeter than losing his virginity. A whole fish sweeter than sex ever was. Ugh. Every line was a coked-up hurl of adjectives. I quietly closed the pdf and got on with my business. Nobody else would scrape the wax out of candleholders or polish the gantry until it was good and ready. I took pride in my work, back then, I tried. The world was an oyster I schlocked love for.

*
**

A man on the door gave me weed brownies, a handful, each the size of dice. I ate them one by one the night before an overdue slumber. Back then, I'd save up sleep for Sundays. What was I supposed to know about dosing? I woke up with my laptop still on my bed, frightened by the proliferation of wiki articles following the topic of will-o'-the-wisps. An unruly, aluminium heat on my belly. My chest became tight with a new excruciating mesh, so I started fantasising about taking my heart out, laying it on a tray, exposing it to any old carcinogen. Disentangling my heart from burning gauze. I'd have some small, inexplicable conversation with its pulse, dredging a nervous semiotics of love. Love as a humour of the organs, etc. The brownies made me sick for hours. Weeks later, I watched the man on the door square up to some skinny dude who made of the night a litany, Fuck off Fuck off Fuck off. Love's iambs overmake us.

Liv said I probably shouldn't swim in the pool. She's not had it swept in years. All sorts might live in there, parasites and a bestiary of minor demons. The thought of a worm taking root inside me, nestling in the depths of my lower intestines; a symbolic, mobius strip of appetite. That was alright. This worm would share my pleasures and pains; it would make me skinny with equivalent greed. It would devour the good bacteria; leave an imbalance I'd notice only after the fact. I'd never had a worm before. We had a cat when I was young and we got the cat wormed. That's all I knew of it, vaguest of process, squirming. I imagined them slithering around like strands of cooked spaghetti, swallowed whole and dissolving in stomach acid. My friend said at a house party in 2005, someone passed a worm in the bathroom. Fuck that. The pool looked eerily green sometimes. I tried not to open my mouth in the water. The worm wrote for me.

We talked about the decline of business in the restaurant, as if it was something funny. You called it a cavern of melancholy. I remember the Christmas I crouched under table 57 and wrote a list of reasons to kill myself. It was some sick joke. I made the smallest nick on my wrist with the steak knife, before hurling it in the cutlery bucket to be washed in the kitchen, wondering where that tiny bead of blood would end up. We needed to get clean of each other. Only on Sundays with the door wedged open, blaring my love's music, do I feel better. This happened when I was twenty-one. Dub thrums remind me of lightly letting my thoughts go. I can't do it anymore. Letting them go as petals, trip step. Feeling too close to a whitey on Sunday, nausea of last night rising. Back then, I took a pleasure in cutting flowers, pushing their stems through the necks of slender vases. Nicking my knuckles on thorns. Misreading the symbolism of chrysanthemums, a bundle for your birthday. I loved walking through the front door, cradling my expensive bouquets. Old men would salute me with nostalgic grimaces. I was one and every woman. All the cellophane felt like ethereal skin, such a waste to throw away. The little stem clippings, screaming, each to each.

Where are you in the cavern of melancholy? I look for your arrival at the bar, every Friday and Saturday night. Everything you do seems freighted by the fact of your lack of speech. Always scrolling away on your phone. I tried things in darkness to make the dark better, snagged your curls at the edge of my vision.

Every bread roll tasted of buttery air.

You ate five that night, chewing the darkness better. I could hear airplanes from my bedroom window. I wanted to wake with you, full in the noon of November. We'd generate the loop form of a new present-tense.

There was that talk at the Autonomous Space about suicide and politics and what would have happened if that philosopher had not—

The air here is so quiet, sometimes I fancy I can hear the succulents whistling.

The butter comes apart on the bread like platelets.

Twin sapphires on my arms from where you'd held me.

*
**

When I was younger, my family went on city breaks. We walked along waterfronts mostly, looking for cheap restaurants. Sometimes we bought food in supermarkets and ate in hotel rooms, sampling foreign tv, crumbs on bedsheets. We street-haunted, kept walking until the backs of our legs burned. Our paces were out of sync, that was the difficulty. My attention was short but my strides were long. I always wanted to buy something: harden a moment. Now I can barely find my purse.

I adored the hoard of hotel breakfast. It was easy then, to just eat everything. I didn't have the buzz in my ears. I would lay down afterwards and read about dissolute women smoking Slims in America.

I learned the word 'food noise' and that you could take a pill for it.

There was that summer of the undiscovered nest, where all these wasps flew into my mother's bedroom. For ages, she didn't do anything about it. Passively hospitable, she let them come in, humming and buzzing about her windowsill where she'd left the glass open a crack for air. Then, with August's vengeance, she sprayed the area over and over. So they'd all be in varying stages of death and dying. Never helping each other, just limply flitting their wings or shivering. They looked so angry and bitter. In their wispy extinguishing, they sounded like distant airspace collisions. She found a few lost in the marshmallow expanse of her duvet or pressed between bed sheets. I couldn't fathom how she slept at night.

*
**

Here we are, beautiful and storm-borne, carrying the flowers of an afternoon. When my friend Theo leaves for Greece, to return no longer, I grow obsessed with that Crosby, Stills, Nash & Young song, 'Our House.' I tell my friend how sad I am about Theo's leaving. He says, but you will always have that flat, where you first...I don't know what flat he means, and neither does he. First what? Origins elude me. I remember the shift where I turned up for work after the rave and I hadn't slept. We had been sitting up in Theo's room, the five of us, listening to 'Lucky' over and over. I poured hot tea on the back of my hand, still stoned. Pursing her lips, the woman I was serving said, "A long day already?"

Honey, we don't even know what a day is.

Theo and I were too shy to do anything.

In the back of my father's car, on the way to a funeral, thinking about being on a roll with death. Never doing straight up searches but Feeling Lucky. The countryside swept back from where I could not cry, the window fronting the fact of my tears. Who was I to cry about this? Let the engine decide. The pollen dragged clear and green and breezy; it was easy to be silent in my father's car, with the window closed. My eyes stung only a little. I had cried out my summer earlier, the first of July, someone's party. I was shaking with the cold and caffeine, painkillers — drunkenness shuddering a well inside me. Sitting on the steps outside, still crying, the boys from before walked by and saw. He was so sweet, the one with the gap between his front teeth, the one who was older. Floppy-haired smoker. He was walking his dog down the high street, and just like that he had seen me.

"Who did this to you?"

I wanted to message him later to say thank you, but the words burned and cloyed and fizzed away. My Facebook remained an interminable blue.

I still see him turning street corners, walking his dog as though the evening hadn't changed.

Warming its way into now…

I become obsessed with the look of orange against cobalt crayola. This was a particular painting in the gallery, one I remembered. A time will come when I can write about the balance of those colours, the way I would recite one emotion just to procrastinate the next. The invigilator was drawing spirals on a tiny notebook with what looked like an expensive, fine-point marker.

I grow too tired and warm for emails.

Remember when you said, with genuine reverie, We write with the same pen! But you do not join up your letters; and I am always writing at a slant, while you strive for perfect verticals.

Wild garlic springs up along the river. It feels luxurious to walk along, buoyed by a promise of diurnal turning; just as in February the crocuses closed at night, were buried in snow. The garlic makes me feel quite well. Already I anticipate bluebells.

*
**

On a plaque, I forget where, I learned about Alyson Shotz's *Mirror Fence* (2003): made of Starphire glass and aluminium to camouflage with its surroundings. A fence that reflected what it kept separate. A fence of green and weather. To leap over would be to cross into a parallel realm, mirror world, my own private cliché of the suburbs. A place we exist and it's peaceful; to be so unsure, to not have shadows.

You said you were drafting a landscape. It wasn't just a case of poring over maps. The dented blaze of a wayfaring stranger. You exacted where I might be, Find My iPhone, a red dot laser traced on wrist. A landscape is mostly a series of lines and transparencies. I wanted to watch the gloaming with you, for we were always passing through surfaces and versions of selves. I felt like you wanted to excavate whatever I'd kept inside me so long; you were that strong. Mostly I watched the songs you listened to on Spotify. Now, I lean into the darkness, retching.

Are you okay, are you okay, are you okay? Sometimes the you slips into we, but only afterwards. When you held me, that Sunday after the party, I had never felt so close to the skin of a quiet oblivion. I did not want to wake up in the sweetness of shock, in my black lace,

I tried to keep you awake. I could taste myself purpling on the edge of your neck.

On the plane, all I could think about was the sheerness of blue. A bluer than blue, 5am sky. Julie Byrne in my head like sonic velvet. We settled into a slumberous drift that brought us down to another country. I walked in the airport for miles.

*
**

Images of mastery in the cards startle. Ruthie would tell me, it's a question of loci, the unfolding potential; my need to feel a symbiotic connection wherever I go. Settling down roots, memories crusted in concrete. They lay over with fresh black tarmac but that only helps preserve the before. Remember I used to dance on the edge of the fresh black tarmac. A concoction of treacle and charcoal. Spiritual core of the person, responsible for waste filtering. It was a deep snow that fucked up the road. They had to lay upon all that had cracked. What a strangeness that seemed, the supermarket shelves without milk or bread or cheese, the headlines filling up with puns about absent loaves. Slushy ice in our footprints. I lived on rice cakes and loved the emptiness, the vaguely glittering night-time panic. What I hated was the trudge required of all walking. The coldness in my kidneys. What I hated was the distance between us. Being always proximate to falling. What I hated was the slow cancellation of our days. Remember when I used to dance on the edge of the sparkling tarmac?

Shooting tequila with my cousin in all the bars of England. This was last summer when I lost myself. The dress, however, was determinedly blue. The colour of duck eggs. I loved it, the wrap effect that folded my breasts. My family kept saying how different

I looked.

My mother used to eat two thick slices of white toast after work, slathered in jam and marmalade. She would read magazines. She would watch the transformative shows on television, the ones about buying up dilapidated flats and making them shiny and new, or decorating gardens with hasty plants. Her hair was thicker. She was buoyed up by a kind of rage at existing. Apart from that, she would take her time.

I took even marmalade for granted. Now I take ages.

I think about kissing you first to last in that living room, in front of everyone, coming up on mandy, a new occasion. How pure that felt, the roar of blood in my ears. Goodbye was a promise I didn't fulfil and now you're gone and I'm sorry. For what? The disasters of kissing and knowing.

Here we are, ad infinitum.

"What is the probability of a second romantic episode?" You spoke in scientific fragments. I found this blog that kept a diorama of screen kisses, marking a shipped couple to well-tethered eternity. The colours were purple and green, saturated with neon and the sense of a new, unending boulevard. There was something in the angles, set against soft focus. Palms on either side of the road, great violet acanthus in gilded pots outside restaurants.

You looped your arm in mine and we both cried *WORK IS OVER.* That night, we bought each other round after round around the sun. Total eros. You left out the wrong door. We opened something up, then shut it down. Our words were clumsy. Our drinks were icy.

I felt clearer. Ours was a vespertine love, almost creaturely. Could it survive the day?

Liv worked in a factory, south of the river. She was a professional. Every surface, she said, was flawless polished steel. You saw your reflection wherever you looked, so it felt like you were building the parts out of pieces of face. Every new car had a bit of her expression left in it: an impress of light once broken.

The cab driver turned on the radio, taking me south. How could The National's 'About Today' just come on, miles away from the past, in the middle of this foreign city? I wept fat silent tears against the window, watching the industrial buildings slip away.

Want to leap over the mirror fence, I texted.

*
**

There in the heart of Berlin: the gallery which was glass and light and everything a myriad language. Everything was glass and light and clarity; even the cafeteria did not smell of food but had the lingering taint of fresh paint and sandalwood. Barely established, the gallery was constantly switching up their exhibited materials, never keeping one thing for more than a month. The few permanent exhibits comprised some passé contemporaries working with abstraction, but it was the still lifes I liked best. The paintings were tiny, the kind of eccentric miniatures you might find in your grandmother's bathroom. You could easily slip one into your coat. Security was passé. The frames were excessive, given that most of the gallery had oversized panels with no frames at all. The still lifes, by contrast, had a distinct aesthetic frame, gilded with whorls and arabesques. I grew obsessed with the micro-worlds they contained. Heavy gold.

Every couple months I'd return to the gallery, mostly to look at these still life paintings. I tried not to bring people with me, lovers or friends or whatever. I was suspicious of anyone else I found in the permanent exhibitions, poring over the same works I did. None of this invited dialogue. What was it about the objects in question, the ones in the painting? It was less the objects in themselves, so much as their collective arrangement. Vape cartridges oozing into clementine gooseflesh, microchips cut like old credit cards to garnish a diner top. Coffee stains on gingham tablecloth. Slices of rotting lemon. Water bottles, pills of Nurofen distributed along stuck reels of FRAGILE tape, a cairn of olives. I looked for intimations of space between things, broke them into bit-parts, the way pornography fragments the human body into orifice and limb and moaning. I looked at the space between handle and spine and the mouthy crushed circle of a teacup, the pale gesture at liquid insides. Reflections, shimmering, shadows. I split everything into presences or gaps, walked around with little sense for my own physicality, precarious mesh of my nerves. It was only when I exited the artificially lit exhibition space, stood instead in the glassy foyer, that I recognised bodily needs. I understood why people reached for their cigarettes. I understood why they sang in cursive.

Sex sometimes fuzzed at my edges, like an aura or warning. Sex was white noise, until it grew pink. Ruthie in my ear like Navi from *The Legend of Zelda*, whispering over and over, your aura is indigo. You are sensitive, dynamic, imperative. I collected such words like charms that didn't quite click on my bracelet; I'd have to artfully wrench their wires to fit.

Hey, listen.

She wore such quantities of eyeliner; so violet as to almost seem black, which looked out of place on her innocent face.

Remember (how could you) the day you gave me that beautiful dark bruise, like a flower unfolding on my thigh. The second you made it was an ice crystal, but it lingered for weeks, refusing to thaw, the only thing I coveted from a night you'd cool to regret.

Drunk again, say love.

At some point during all this, Liv had her pool serviced. Men came with nets and special powders that smelled of lemons and chlorine and rain. In the eerie, perpetual dusk, it glowed a brighter indigo. Even she would swim in it now. She paid a fortune.

What shifted between us? A glacial shelf.

I stayed awake for a blue moon, but it was covered with cloud. Such is the general effect of my city. Missing the vision, I pored over climate forums, waiting for people to upload high-res photographs, watching the live-feed comments unfurl on YouTube. The blue in the pictures was never quite what I expected. An Interminable Blue. The colour of international reputation. I wanted a cold kind of local, sultry cobalt. After the reading in December, I walked through the park in the dark and admired a moonbow. It seemed to go on for days, radiating this protective galaxy. Months later, there would be a blood moon, its magnetism recalibrating my entire cycle.

We bonded over posting the same moon again.

*
**

Sometimes Google makes you add actual words to your 'personal dictionary.' As in, clearly pre-existing signifiers. How funny to think of owning, personally, a word like 'Fire' or 'Hand.'

I wish there was some way of accessing this personal dictionary, a box of collated words. Beautiful nouns, adjectives and verbs without context. I met a poet friend who sat on a hay bale with me in some exhibition of the blanched pastoral and told me whenever she reads a book she notes all the words that she doesn't know on the back page, in pencil. Poets are such obsessives. I did this with the most peculiar novel I have ever read. What resulted was a shopping list of qualities. The words I'd never heard before:

Rubescent

Cubbies

Sorcellated

Lateritious

Stucco

Unisonous

Augury

Bequeathal

Butte

Distention

Griseous

Demesne

Pulmonary

Egesta

Cyanosis

Clamjamfry

Maremma

Enfilade

Cronelate

Vistae

Augur

Equidistant

Contiguous

Lashy

Planar

Antipodal

Cyclorama

Atrophies

Pergola

Ducal

Enmauvened

Recondensing

Defervesced

Integument

This novel, my word source, was written by an architect. Or a vulture. What kinds of swarming or swooning are involved? I like to read when I'm hungry. To make use of waste. The novel is arranged in sort of textual plats or grids, but I read it mostly while walking, having little time to read things in static locations. Plot offered its sky burial and I took it with zeal. The transition into spring slipped by as I devoured the paragraphs. There was a new motion imbued within the structure, owing to my pace and the slippages of gold light and green around me. Scenes acquired a fluid transition. This was the canal, aligned with pylons; there the motorway, adjacent screens of scrolling sky.

This patterned land, our flattened plans.

The gallery was also arranged like a grid. There were no complicated corridors or winding stairwells; it was so easy to find things. Everything had its turn or parallel. A city inverted, its fuel distilled.

The gallery as metropolis. I was reminded of the grid systems of Toronto, Philadelphia, Glasgow; places I knew intimately, on-screen, or through word-of-mouth at least. In other galleries, there was the problem of aporia: sometimes I'd turn a corner and find myself back in the room where I started, without realising how this happened. What turns had I made, without meaning, to get here. Why was I so afraid of arrows? Galleries rarely invite the desire for linear development, blind progress. You are always in some sense oscillating, thrown back, milling between the one and the other. Between walls. There was a sense of being watched and watching; the invigilators here were particularly vigilant. Sometimes I'd observe them picking the fine, manicured cuticles of their nails, or shuffling papers in their hand, adjusting a wristwatch. *I dial my life backwards and forwards in time.* I once saw one staff member politely tap a man on the shoulder, escorting him to the side of the room where a small alcove provided a stack of information brochures, warning signs. I tried to figure out why. Had he been crying? Tears corrupt pale ambience. It's not that the gallery was affectless per se, so much as boastful of its own restraint. The most gorgeous, trembling images were placed in such a way to mute your reaction. They'd be surrounded by trivial works, tin cans and abstracts, explained away with poorly written plaques or captions. You were supposed to glance and move on. Maybe the feeling would come back later, as I mulled over crumbling pastries in my hotel room. I'd halt at the suddenness of that cardinal red, splashing the corner of a room, the very yellow squares in a tablecloth, the unnatural quantities of blue that filled a scene with shadow. I could hardly explain my reaction, but that didn't matter. It was more about the way things slotted, edged and clicked together. Or it was about the sullen persistence of the visible stroke.

I have always been sensitive to colour. Transitioning through puberty, my body awash with hormones, I could not wear colour at all. The rainbow garms of my childhood incited migraines. Sparse images that remain from that era show a girl clad awkwardly in black, allergic to sun. I glowered in all photographs, I hardly slept; so even my eyes looked black. Everyone asked, are you a goth? Do you fuck the dead? I would look at the sky and say yes to everything.

Sometimes, I would see a plane.

The first colour I learned to apply to my eyes was lilac. It was Hallowe'en but I wanted to be light. I sat in someone's car and used the rearview mirror.

So this is what it was, she looked at me
bruisingly, to speak to ghosts.

For a few years, your heart was a sugar cube
stuck in my throat.

I swore my colours would be cool from now on.

The gallery was tiled with squares, another grid structure, all in different shades of white and grey with the odd one in yellow (ochre) or pastel blue. They were almost vacuum sealed into each other, a seamless array of lines which betrayed their exactly measured shapes. I used to work in a restaurant where the tiles in the bathrooms were always coming loose. They were black and white tiles of different sizes. I guess all the Friday night stilettos had eventually prised them from their cement beds, so they'd tremble as you walked over them, as you pressed your feet into the ground, weary from a shift or the booze. Those tiles were iconic. My colleague, one Hogmanay, finished her shift by taking one of the biggest tiles, peeling it loose, and shattering it on the street outside. She gave no context for this action. It splintered into many pieces, one of them hitting a parked car and setting off the alarm. We giggled and disappeared into the dark, which was generally the arc of our stories.

Why did some galleries lead you back to the start, while others offered parallel labyrinths with easeful navigation? Why did some invite disappearance, while others insisted on the presentness of everything?

Once, I had a date in the gallery café. She was herself an aspiring painter with an Instagram full of studio visits. One of the Slade lot, class of whenever. Her name was Ada. I liked the white dungaree cut-offs in the photos with the blue paint flecking her thighs. To our date she wore an ugly grown-up blazer. We smashed overpriced salads and talked about troubles with housemates. This led to ranting catharsis. Darkly, she threatened to move to Margate. I laughed, said I'd been feeling blue — that I loved Margate, which could be true. She gave me a list of her jealousies. I asked if I could write them down. She laughed at me actually doing this on a napkin and I think it goaded her further. She said, "only if we don't sleep together." She said, "I will tear this up if we sleep together."

What if I hide it?

I can easily piece together
things that are torn apart.

Her jealousies, tossed and dressed:

Jealous of the light in Olafur Eliasson

Jealous of the first person to crochet a snowflake

Jealous of Escherian memes

Jealous of Lily Bunney's pointillism

Jealous of the crepuscular in Constable

Jealous of babies in frescos

Jealous of Vermeer's milkmaid

Jealous of Ada, Countess of Lovelace

Jealous of her ex's poor circulation

Jealous of shadows

Jealous of Dadu Shin's ballpoint drawings

Jealous of girls who experienced the era of blingee firsthand, who vajazzled for real

Jealous of spirals

& so on.

When I think of her, the avatar glows blue.

What about you?

Such obsessive checking I have been round and round in my life, waiting for the green light to come on against you. There were times I wished to throw my phone off a bridge. Is there a word for that? Mostly I withheld my reply for later. I drew my breath for the duration of a sunset, a sunset I'd seen on the internet. It was like I was waiting for myself to muster the words, pale supplements, not even waiting for yours; what was more maddening?

I felt like a poet caressing photons. Like someone left the sun turned on overnight, like love was just the light on your iPhone — an

adjustable brightness.

How many times would you say it: "Please can I ask the unspeakable…"

After the party, we stopped narrative again and again. Everyone else had left. I would get dressed, I would tie up my hair.

Just when you were getting closer.

And what did happen?

It was possible to say: "I love you, I've forgotten the time of day."

It was possible to give me that look and put on Suzanne Vega.

Your roommate was distracted, tidying the kitchen.

We snuck out to a restaurant where they served us artichoke: entire, splayed, complex to fathom. We eked its many hearts.

You said it was unspeakable to ask for silence. For nothing. So I would turn a book into a phone to talk through it.

So we didn't fuck.

I cried that I was changing.

What if we saw ourselves five years from now in the silent club scene of the grieving movie? We'd have aged into anonymity.

Shame grew upon me like a skin. What ghost purpose did I serve us — and what was our life? Initially I clung to the complicated deliciousness of how it was the first time. The sight of leaves on trees startled me into last year's recognition. The nameless trees by the river. How time passed, the melting of winter; my heart glanced hopefully through uncertain glass, a digital expense. I kept to my word; never telling anyone. The scenes played over and over, slowly morphing as your chemical presence in my body altered. The rush might recede, biting my lips, pushing up tricky inclines.

I would become a scrubbed entity, if it killed me.

I would still get away with lilac. It brings out the greener flecks in my irises. The first time we got high together, dabbing white powder from a stamp-sized baggy, we spent about an hour looking into each other's eyes, saying nothing and then everything. I realised, then, that yours were green. Unexpectedly green, not obnoxiously. Green as moss is. You said it was something you were proud of, your green green eyes. The way they tricked you into realising, gradually, that they were green. You looked boyish and content, admitting that. Mine are blue-grey, colours of the sea; they change into green sometimes, as in a mood ring. If you're cool.

What do you want or fear the most?

The opposite of gold is indigo.

We were born under different suns. We curled around one another all June; the warm day was outside but we were in here with the others and sweetly blooming.

Your absence changed me.

I think about the indigo pool in Berlin. Similar kinds of rippling. I'm only an athlete when I'm drinking. Running along empty roads at night, I imagine myself pounding away the shame. I am back in the aftermath of an accident. At night, we overlap in dreams.

In the morning, our cocktail of cortisol.

You know, most of our interaction was goofball humour, flutters of hilarity. I'd relay what you said to a friend, and he'd call it Luxurious Patter. Solid gold jokes. I liked that a lot. I don't want anyone to think we were less than a lightness; the sheen of something substantial underneath; a mutual acceleration, like sucking in bright quantities of air when no one else was looking. Our eyes would meet and we'd burst into laughter, but even afterwards something within me stayed glistening. I nourished it, softly mulling over our words in all those instances of walking home.

There's a line I can't shake that's been with me for years.

Remember when we stood in the lashing rain so drunk... we were trying to get cash but you were telling me about your family, expectations and the like, and I was so content then to erase myself of anything beyond being here and there, your interlocutor. My wet hair stuck to my neck, how you looked in your orange beanie. With you I did not need another thought. I took £20 out and spent it on empty calories, plastic cups of beer, just to preserve the space in which we could blur and dance and make blue.

We'd go outside to smoke and talk in the quiet. Strangers would misinterpret our intimacy for the couple form, with praises. We'd let them bless our future in exchange for cigarettes.

Time passed, pound for pound. The currency changed and there was so much of it still lying around, extinct and paper. I kept finding bits of tinsel in the carpet, from Christmases gone by. Sometimes I'd look into the summer sky and the tinsel bits would flicker at the edge of my vision. It was possible I'd spent too long in that flat. I could not muster the energy to change. I developed migraines.

Sometimes I'd feel flat, with something gathering within me, pale and yet temporarily present, insistent on never rising. The bubbles that form in a glass of water, left too long in daylight.

What passed was the lore and logic of songs and albums. Just a sentence to explain each one, little intimations of critical poetry. We framed our lives with songs, that was the trick of it. Remember when we both agreed we were from another planet, how our parents had not believed us until we insisted. Sometimes the power of insisting alone.

You were stacking crates of glasses from behind the curtain and heard me talking about growing old, about looking back at my youth. It is so arduous, to feel on the cusp of things. A few of us were talking about the age of our souls before the dinner rush earlier. The younger your soul, the more open you are to perceiving evidence of the spirit realm. My mother always said I was an old soul; she said she'd known this since the day I was born. I often feel weary, inclined to the feel of this all as epoch. The last thing I heard you shout, while I was leaving with my coat and keys, was "Maybe if you keep cycling, you'll look the same when you're forty."

I push myself harder on the road now, sun on my face, collecting muscles and freckles, shaving the years.

One time I was leaving a party early with the phrase, I'm gonna make tracks. This boy I knew, a sort of musical prodigy, thought this meant I had plans to enter a studio, lay down some music. He was so out of it he'd probably have believed me. My leaving was a composition. I watched him play drunk jazz fingers on the coffee table, clumsily rolling joint after joint. Today, I can't picture his teeth, his expression. Only his hair as it was then, girlish and long, the thinness of his wrists and those long pianist's fingers, the skin on the back of his hands dry and fine as lace... I was so elated at the fact of what nearly happened. You had been at the party. Proximity. The fact of my leaving, my lips stained dark with tannins. "Well, are you going to?" someone asked. The next party we were at together, I found the other boy. I sat between him and his flatmate, holding a little sparkler till it fizzled to a crisp and smelled of gunpowder. I was in perfect safety.

During that time, there was or was not at every afters a man called Tristram, who had long, side-swept hair and always sat in the corner, playing chess and snorting ketamine from a custom glass phial as he took his opponent's every pawn.

You were my own midsummer dissociative.

Basement flats always had a strange effect on me. Something about the lack of air. The curious plants that grew in damp profusion. The swamp of bodies.

Walking home, I was always unsure of the routes to take. There seemed too many possibilities, a thrill in the length or cut, as though the mesh of that grid was the expanded version of a notable dress. A gauzy wonder I'd worn as a girl.

I kept thinking of a lyric from this song about Ohio. Navigating somebody else's heartache: warm canals, clear blue pools. Except he puts the blue at the end, it's the point in that clause. When everything feels dead-end, restless and regrettable, there's the blue. Burning blue the unsayable. And I love his highway, his endless lovers, his angel embodied geography. His excuse for being absent, I can't say.

My sleepless eyes look indigo lately.

Pray for subsidence. I listen to podcasts recorded by people recovering from earthquakes. They are talking about being inside the earthquake. Writing from a position of shaking. I imagine time trembling around me, knocking things from the walls. It doesn't seem much good for anything else right now.

When I think about you too much I am inside the earthquake. I am an embarrassment of disasters. My voice trembles and what's within threatens to brim over: all around becomes a slow white noise and I am nauseous, desperate to expel what I cannot.

In various European cities, I'd hire a bike and get around that way. It was a good method to cheat the imperative to sightsee, to dwell upon detail. Mostly I'd focus on lights and sound and traffic, the unruly movement of human bodies. Every city has its unique arboreal networks of madness. Every city gets too hot.

I'd end up avoiding the museums, skirting the rivers, drinking in bars where men in suits became gradually undone, sloshing their beards with beer until their faces stank and their breath was everywhere. I missed being in bars where folk drank whisky, spoke quietly of what. I still miss the ill-advised last orders of malt. Somebody order me a Bowmore.

I miss how back home it was totally acceptable to walk into a bar at 2pm and order a double or three. Here, they thrust a menu in your direction.

At the concert, she screeched: "This one's for everyone who couldn't make it tonight. God bless y'all in your sickness." I decided then I'd fashion a new vitriol for punk rock. It left unpleasant blisters in my ears which I'd try to pick out like morse code, ringing and ringing for days afterwards. This time, we left the room and hung out at the bar, watching the bubbles rise in other people's pints.

What does it mean to leave the world alone? Does it require a word? What is it to leave the word?

I missed Liv, who was always making me salads. She tossed lettuce leaves with oil and vinegar and lemon, she slashed tomatoes till their juice came out seedy and runny and red, sprinkled fistfuls of parsley into enormous wooden bowls, which she mushed up with quinoa and the fragrance of silence. She could do extravagant things with radishes, knew a deli that sold good capers. She seasoned everything with so much pepper I'd be sneezing afterwards. We ate on the patio, by the indigo pool. It never seemed to rain in Berlin, but it was often overcast. Liv served her salads with glasses of white wine, which I did not drink so much as seem to drown inside.

*
**

After work, I'd come back down again. Come back to wherever you were. As if you were waiting on some hammock, sipping carnelian glasses of bourbon, and not actually whiling the hours away in the glow of your too-white screen, your milky tea.

In Berlin, my brother and I walked for hours and hours through industrial estates, along byways. We weren't looking for anything particular: more a sense of general, digressing motion to complement our wayward conversation. It had been a while since we'd picked apart our lives so mutually. What did I hold back? I was at the brink of new things then, unaware of a coming depression. It was June, the sky impossibly blue. I did not yet know the phrase 'my luteal phase.' There was this sort of oasis, adjacent to the motorway. I drank a long cold gin, three times the price of a beer. I have never learned to like beer, but I try to in your company. As in, will sip cheap lager for kicks at six in the morning, narcotic milk. There was a hammock in this oasis, which my brother fell asleep in as I worried the frays of my denim skirt, watched the traffic passing. There seemed no need to take photos; there was too much light altogether.

How far away the Berlin of those days. My brother, now researching agriculture, of all things. My brother, stuck to the prairie, smoking the sky away.

I press the ball of my palm too hard as I type; blood from the bike accident stains the surface of my warm, aluminium laptop.

*
**

At a party, it got to maybe nine in the morning and the mandy was wearing off and we were melting into separate introspections of ourselves, a point in the party that scares me and for which I often compensate with delirious, apophenic chatter — trying to connect everything, tragically with language. Some daytime politician was on in the background, muted (it was a Sunday; routine TV seemed imperative). A stranger took my phone, which was connected to speakers, and put on a certain song. The television dissolved, so it was only the people in the room; for once I thought nothing of images. I was so startled with the rightness of that choice, my love of that song and the absolute melancholy attached to it, that I embraced him right there and then, with tears in my eyes. I did not speak for the whole song, but lay back on the sofa, leaning against his shoulder and absorbing the rainbow harmonics of pop's fossil finest. Where warm before, my body became marmoreal in the moment, that weirdly spiritual quality of stone. Then we talked awhile, words I've forgotten, warmed over.

We became friends after that, mostly messaging at five in the morning. Nobody leaving their twenties ever seems to stay up late anymore. At some point, they all fall into a regular sleeping pattern; while I lagged, chasing the night birds. I went to bed with you one afternoon. We were so calm and then suddenly upset. We had barely touched one another. I walked home with guilt flared in every muscle, couldn't find my way out of your neighbourhood. I walked in so many circles. My phone dead, people being sick on the last train; the shortest journey that suddenly felt so long. Horrors of Sunday. What was it my mother said when she saw me, later on? It's funny, I only recall that she wanted to brush my hair. But every pore of my body felt gluey with you. I slept and the hours I lost to sleep were miles, miles, miles.

Remember when I came out the pool, nude, my skin printed all over with leaves, and Liv said I looked like a mermaid. She was such a pain mystic. Did she say pain? I was scared of the hornets.

Something out of a movie. I was swimming to fix my bruised and battered knees.

You see I came off my bike, quite badly. It was May and I was in my hometown, so excited to just be cycling. A green world rushed behind me, until I was skimming through concrete metropolis. It was a bank holiday, late, an absence of traffic. I flipped properly over on a kerb and banged my head in the process. There were two shreds of skin missing from my left knee, but all I could think about was fixing the chain, preserving my freedom. My fingers blackened with oil as I tried to latch the chain back on. It was only when I got home that I realised my leg was streaming with blood. My hair all flattened by the helmet; I looked positively garish. My wound purpled red for days and grew glossy with the grease of Germolene.

A woman in the distance, mowing her lawn. The crenellated edges of a canvas, its shock of crimson. I don't know the limits to what you can do with oils. There seems an infinitude to that kind of smearing, like channelling the unspent grease and mulch of the skin's near surface. What the body secretes in longing. I fall asleep on city buses, contemplating vague intimations of art. Why did she cut out those chunks along the edge of her canvas? Why did the woman want her grass shorter? Why do we shell out expensive card transactions in salons where they billow our hair into clipped submission, mirrorball shiny?

I stopped smoking after the last haircut. I stopped smoking, even when I was drinking. I arrived a little late, often for the sake of impression. When people said I smelled good, I suppose I lit up with my own fresh presence; I reassured myself on the topic of occupying physical space. Coconut shower gel, coconut oil, coconut scent from The Body Shop — the same flavour I had worn for a decade or more, hinting at a prior, fantasy life spent reclining on islands, coveting palms. I would carry the little glass bottle around in my schoolbag, I would bring it back from the city to the prairie. It covered the lunchtime smell of menthols. At school, I used to know a girl from the islands. She wore coconut perfume from dawn to dusk and now she works in finance. We used to crush on each other, though boys were our nexus.

I wonder what happens to people when they give up cigarettes. Do the structures of their brain change enough to alter who they are? What kinds of chemical persona have we been together? Nicotine entwined after all.

There are so many cats in the parks of Berlin. Drug dealers and feline companions. All of them sharing a greenness. I grow frustrated with my lack of language. I brush the cigarette scar on the side of my wrist. Cats occupy errant coordinates, poised for rest or kill.

Did you think with that whisky I was trying to seduce you? Funny thought, on the seats outside in the cold, passing around this miniature bottle. Where it all began, that freezing November…

Hello sleepover, morning glow when everyone else still snores and tosses. Little ocean of youth. Wake up to DVD menu screen: eerie music, ersatz flickers, icons drifting. My body writhes and isn't mine. *First to wake and last to sleep.*

A computer screen can never quite approximate the colour of indigo — its spectral quality, its luminosity, its residue of the sun or twilit tropical. Here, between realms. Never quite the screen of death. Not even the screen of desuetude.

Those early days of discovery, we drank enormous bottles of cherryade laced with vodka. We did this on buses (I won't dox the numbers), so every lurch and curve of the road was treacherous. I was not sick. I was never sick except on purpose; I could stuff a whole fist down my throat. I gave good blowjobs, said my little solar eclipse. I was texting some boy about the possibility of buying a lime green jumper from a high street sale. He was so adamant it would suit him and I agreed, swept inside the wrath of his enthusiasm. All I wanted was for him to be at this party, emanating the fast-food thrills of the past. I spent the night mostly playing with my friend's cats, curling their bunny-soft ears, following them out into the garden which backed upon a river, a river drenched in moonlight. I let that boy take my femininity. I looked for torsos that might warm me, but none seemed enough. I was a cat like that. The cats were jealous of each other and withdrew into the shadows if I picked one over the other. I'd come home the next day, my skin a crochet of feline scars. For affection scratches, a script of blood-drawn language. I scooped the fur in my arms and did not sleep all night. Nobody watched me. I'd melt into solvent girlishness.

These dreams, Emily Brontë wrote in Catherine's voice, have 'gone through and through me, like wine through water, and altered the colour of my mind.' Every time I write I too am spreading the liquid. Diffusion is not disappearance. The trees are not right this year; I can't hear the birds. There is one tree which looks to be overcome with ghosts. It went silver overnight and then died from the inside. I press a tender lump just below my stomach, feel its acorn of painful swell. Depression is a hollow. I press my fingers into a lenticel and breathe with my ghost tree. The bruise, the bruise, the bruise; the blood mottling hot and cold beneath. The silence you left changed the world, the world already out of sync. I had to be my own heartwood.

But still I have a night or two. We sipped from a bottle of tonic wine, burned with caffeine and medicinal purple.

I dream of you in gradients, gardens.

The way we were your other life.

*
**

At the bus stop, the second one in the town, this boy I'd only just met taught me what fritters were. Those battered delights, melt in your mouth Fridays. I felt drizzled and crisped by his sorceries. The way he held me, like he was a pontil and I was just glass, molten and plasmic in his grasp, so he could fashion from my skin a new language, little pellicles of my flesh which were warm, semisoft, morphing with hieroglyphs; but cold when he left me, blank and hard as hide. To frit, to make into frit. Remember when I fell over, skidded on the asphalt, so all those shards of silica and grit lodged in my palm? To frit: to fright. What feels lit when you click play, when you eat blueberries straight from the fridge and kiss me.

*
**

I am no one maybe, no-one, a withdrawn effect of lugubrious light.

The lift at work keeps breaking. Once, there was a hostage situation, where the doormen would not let the men trapped inside out until they had stopped swearing, until they had apologised. There was a lot of metallic banging. I had never seen such intensity of masculinity trapped between two floors.

Is this the same feeling as being stuck in an earthquake? No.

A colleague and I concocted a conspiracy about the origins of all these lift breakages. There's a lab at the base of the building, where someone is making clones from hundreds of trapped customers. So they keep leaking out, so they are the same genetic etcetera. I have seen you before, and you and you. Imagine your personality spliced to identical fragments. Would I miss you more — in your pieces?

Once, this customer broke her nail, pushing a button on the lift. I watched her lower lip wobble as she explained the situation to me, a wee shard of shiny pink plastic pinched between two fingers. We gave her a free glass of Prosecco, we sat her in a plush chair before encouraging her silence. She cried like crazy.

The anonymous woman's soft, buttery voice murmuring down the telephone: *please hang up and try again.* I used to dream about this, waking up breathless in the abyss of night — as if the missed connection released a swarm of ghosts.

Of course, she was a cerberus guarding the unspeakable.

In the morning I am everyone's hunger artist.

What I do now is so different to before.

Whole quantities of correspondence I reserve for you. Who am I writing back for, and what comes hurtling to the room where I sit here, waiting then starving? A maelstrom of absence catches, I can press it deep against the bounds of my belly.

I used to get so sick I would hide in the stalls and dream of a plane of blackness, a long line that could swallow me. It was like zooming into the space between tiles in a grid, making a depth, sinking.

My sad departed digital ghost. The buddleias climb through the railings, exploding their purple all July.

You said you loved me, twice, when you were drunk at the disco. You would do this again years later. We were there for no reason. For a moment, you laid your hand on my thigh. You kept looking away, as though this was necessary. You made me feel like a modest alien. We bundled ourselves into warmth.

The light here is green and gold. I still sleep with two duvets, layered on top of each other. The green clings to the spider plant and the gold. An effect of something outside catching quite beautifully on the cheap IKEA light. There will be a time when I look back on this room as quaint. When every object holds a little memory I can pull into my lap at virtual distance, gradually unravel the stories and feelings. Feel each twinge of pain and crinkle. Right now, things are too close. Why does it hurt, the spiralling uncontrollable feeling? To have a 5am conversation with you is all I need, but now I cannot stay up past three. Plans to sink pints and wake with the starlings, my only measurements.

I dream of him sitting in a library which is not quite a library and the very next day I bump into him at a pedestrian crossing, waiting for the light to change. He is dressed so smart I hardly recognise him. He says he is going to the library with a friend.

Liv rolls the neatest whitest cigarettes. Her breath is so perfect I envy her lungs.

These late late late ones. There's a gap in the hedgerows near my childhood home where I used to wedge my body and watch for the sheep coming over the hill. The air smelled of toxic botanicals and rain, even when it was summer and sunny and it wasn't even raining. The sheep brought their own smell. I had a crush on the boy who herded them with a black-and-white dog whose name was Maisie. I never did catch the boy's name. He was too old for me to have known him from school. Even from a distance, I could see there were holes in his jeans. I had walked past him in town once or twice, heavy techno leaking through his earbuds, mud on his jacket.

My favourite smell is hawthorn.

I know the boy's name now. I opened my local newspaper on a whim years later; saw he'd been killed in a motorbike accident. There was an interview with his mother. She needed someone new to tend the farm, her eyes in the photograph were so misty, they were hardly there. I thought of the gauze which bound up unreachable parts of the road.

The cloudy gin they sell at the riverside bar. I drink it cool and straight with ice, cracked off the glacial shelf. I think of the indigo pool in Berlin.

*
**

Liv's little texts arrive on my phone at all hours of the night like perfect vignettes. She is always spilling out of bars and taxis, texting me as she texts everyone, constantly. She is up for days, sending me YouTube videos of music nobody listens to anymore. She is sometimes manic, but never tragically so. I watch very sincere young men purr over guitars and stare at their feet, until it is too gross to watch altogether. I click on the selfie she's sent me, her saucer eyes and newly-dyed hair. I zoom into where her pores become pixels and I'm listening to the denouement of some other track, listless and strange. I have a job to do but I avoid it, the glare of the spreadsheet. She is always online, poor Liv. She is always telling me to come to Berlin. Always new things. Same old phrases. *So ist es halt.* I can't think of her face without thinking of the white of a screen, text scrolling across it like a news ticker. She sends selfies from the factory, her face split across the glass of several surfaces, simultaneously.

She said she once rescued a cat from her pool. Perhaps it had leapt from the building, trying to cover the space between walls, and misjudged the distance. No other reason why cats would jump into water, surely. But I pondered whether the cat had suicidal ideations, whether it shared a sort of German introspection. The Werther effect; could it appeal across generations, species? O my dear, suicidal kin. Perhaps the cat had enough of the metropolitan smog, perhaps it was suffering from unrequited love. All of that sorrow is such a bore. Did it appreciate Liv fishing its poor body, tail-first, from the pool? I imagined the cat hacking up lungfuls of indigo water, glaring at her in spite. No gratitude at all. That's cats for you, taking for granted the fact of life — having more lives ahead of them.

Probably the cat story was completely untrue.

It was Liv I first told about the pills. She clasped my hand, ever so preciously. She poured jasmine tea from the kettle. She asked nothing more of me.

Except, what was that mark on my wrist?

My veinbow.

We were walking in the blue dark after midnight, near full moon, a little white moth trailing us home.

I used to line them up in pretty white rows, the pills, thinking of Liv with her pretty white cigarettes. You could only buy them abroad, carefully wrapped. You couldn't buy them here anymore, not like that. Everything that happened to me while travelling I took home; I could line up into pretty white sentences of some other person.

I couldn't possibly be responsible for people or chemicals.

Sometimes I look at my life as a catalogue of men who blur into phantasms misaligned with their purpose. Remember when the chain came off my bike and my fingers were smeared in black black oil and I kept rubbing the oil on the rain-sodden grass, trying to get off what failures stained me. I could not cycle home without a stranger staring. My presence on the streets invited this refracted attention, as if every face was waiting to tell me something.

People are always waiting to tell women something. They appear from the shadows, are wheeled out by fate, just to tell you something. Often the cause is wholly inane.

I still often dream of that plane of blackness. Is it a highway, a line of text seen from the sky, a strip of geophysical feature?

I think of the fire marsh prairies, with the sun extinguished and nothing alight except for the tips of the silver birches. Somebody set them aflame in summer. Somebody had the match, they must have. Burned in the vibrant silence of lightning bugs. Gasoline and diesel. Cam was always striking matches, flicking sparked ones in the grass in lieu of talking. Everything around him would quietly smoulder.

"I teach Music lessons, you know. If you give me a call, I can teach you how to play any instrument you want."

This random guy folded a piece of paper, decorated with WordArt like the A4 printout of a hallowed school disco, two decades ago. It stuck to my grimy, oil-slick fingers and I stuffed it in my rucksack, as if for safekeeping. I cried all the way home, on and off, hoping I would not bump into anyone. I was tired of talking to strangers. I wanted it to rain. I felt hateful.

I was waiting for the green light, that little symbol to show that you'd come online. It wasn't like I was going to talk to you or anything. I just needed to know you existed, somewhere, a figment of green.

Resolving my body in anonymous stations, I was trying to forget you existed, crumbling blueberry muffin between my fingers. Just enough amnesia so that the next time I saw you it would be extra delicious: that fallback into memory and presence, the amazing reality of your hair and skin, your eyes like two forests, twinning.

How many rooms have flushed my little white pills? Were they for darkness, sadness or allergies? How many times lain on bright bathroom floors, counting the smooth white tiles?

In Liv's living room I sat and watched a spider traverse her sordid carpet. Its legs were so thin it looked as though a small black dot was moving of its own accord, gliding towards some unseen exit. A receding period. I recall the light from the nightclub, tiny blue lasers, how they scored our skin with temporary presence. To be stung by blue, scattered with turquoise freckles. Borne by spiders.

I watched her make out with someone taller than god.

I walked around alone all night, so she could take this person home.

We used to pay the wild cab drivers to arrive at a sunset. Just say it like that, lisping the dialogue, asking for a shoreline, a horizon or viewpoint. Tell them you are writing a novel and sigh as if that were the hardest thing in the world. I added pink blusher to my cheeks and waited for the sea-wind to blizzard it clean into peach. Here you were. You sent me a record of hazy stoner rock, left out your usual emojis, sounded sincere as hell. My data was dwindling and I could not listen; the wind was in my ear and the idea of the album was sufficient. Imagine you burned the wind onto vinyl, transparent oil etched with these cool, aeolian hieroglyphs. I'd lie awhile listening to the zephyrous crackles. I'd tip my drivers extravagantly.

I'd not reply except for this breath.

Nowadays, you have to have a fixed destination. Google your own goddamn sunset.

Can we do something mischievous again?

I could put myself through every scenario. Giving you a backie on my bike, glaring at headlights. We radiated so much blue.

Gold aluminium frosted with sweat.

You said just take it; it's the perfect elixir. You knew nothing, then, of my ailments. I was finding it hard to prise myself away from the sheets. The sound of a can cracked open at six in the morning. No wisdom forsooth is pain, or something.

The world felt then like a rash; it was too much of everywhere, too much implicit potential, itching.

You see, the Wordsworths often rose after ten or eleven. They made a fashion of idleness. They drank excessive quantities of tea and dawdled their afternoons away on long walks in the hills. Intermittent dosages of sweet caffeine. At any one time, Dorothy or William would be feeling sickly. Then not, then bright and walking. Coleridge crying beneath his lime tree. These were the necessary conditions for a good, strong wandering poetry. An ambient hormonal pocket of paradise. The way Dorothy loved the lines; did she know how her prose fed into them? I cast out my rhymes, waiting for the click that signalled return. I tried to breathe deeply. I drank my earnest lager.

Made the mornings into innocence more squalid.

*
**

Last autumn, I visited the gallery again. There was a room filled with fuzzy television sets, the light dimmed to amethyst, a trip-hop soundtrack eking out the background errata of a desiccated fin de siècle. Wherever you looked, another fuzzy screen. I swear this exhibit had been done before, I'd seen it before. Maybe abroad. The only difference was the trip-hop. There were no lyrics, just endless, downtempo beats. I felt nauseous, as though someone had swerved my orientation — just one gaze had done it, upended. I realised the static of each screen was slightly slanted, so it appeared as though the images were about to slide or dip. I visited the gallery alone. When I finally left, Liv was waiting outside, biting fat chunks from an apple, sliding her fingers up and down her phone. I thought of the juice from the apple, seeping into each pixel, bled through the expensive glass of her screen.

Liv was my favourite incarnation of Eve.

The leaves stirred around me, bristling from the lime trees in the parking lot. They were so perfectly aligned I felt sick again, thinking of television sets. I was suspicious: the whole world had started to slant, then gape. Every step felt acclivitous; my thighs were shaking. The apple Liv handed me, fresh from her bag, had a tiny hole bored all the way through it. She said that was lucky, or something. She refreshed her timelines once a minute.

Navigating the grid to get out the gallery seemed an interminable experience. It was pretty much the same as browsing, where everything associatively swirls and sticks to the sweat of your skin, the uncertain smiles around you. Do people smile authentically when looking at art?

Sometimes I take little notes on my phone. The extra asceticism of refraining from walking on escalators.

Philosophy Queen in the dream between us.

You referred to the homeward hour of 4am as a kind of twilight that stopped you from sleeping. There is a lovely Orcadian word for this, the night hours of midsummer where dusk slips through dawn without the dark's exception: *grimlins*. I pictured you far away, tossing and turning after work, rich in your summer sweat. I was so bummed out in the nothingness of my own body, lying in bed in the cooler glow of proto-dawn, that I forgot how it felt when we held each other through the afternoon. The thought makes me nauseous; I'm sorry for how much I wanted it.

*
**

Once upon being a child I decided I'd one day buy my mother a diamond. It would be synthetic, ethical. Then it grew too late to picture her, brushing her fingers over the plush blue case as she lifted the white, disinterested stone.

Why this diamond? I wanted to incarnate how hard it was for both of us, being in the world.

Nowadays, I imagine my mother at the end of telephones. Hello, hello.

Talk to me, always.

Hope hardly grows in these old suburban gardens. When visiting your father I am elsewhere and so sorry. He leaves the teabag in; he cannot look at me. The house smells of lager and stale electricity.

Imagine me, pressed against a trampoline.

Magical anything.

One night all the work folk were out clubbing then back at some flat with endless lines, talking shit about our bosses and kitchen politics. Conversation snapped around me. When my jaw started going, I chewed my arm. This was because I wanted to kiss you, lots and lots, but couldn't in front of the others. Remember the first time we made a decision about this. Let Marlene have some gum, said someone. There was nothing there the next day, no marks but the rings beneath my eyes. Purple circles. A pain in my skull. A noise complaint.

Coming down, I felt the world all of Mercury.

You are the glint of sunlight, tweaked between the fronds of a palm in the glasshouse of the Botanic Gardens. I suspect such palms should grow on the prairie in considerable abundance. Skirting the edge where they didn't. Could I too be a native species of somewhere? Liv bought special powder for her face; she called it Visage. I think it was full of palm oil. It was supposed to reflect light just so, to make you particularly photogenic. She shone in all her photos, but I suspect this was less to do with surfaces. Nicotinamide, Tranexamic and Azeleic Acid. The bars she preferred were both posh and mellow; they sold cocktails in indulgent jugs without straws, so inevitably as she poured it was me who glugged all the ice. Heavy sloppy ice in my glass. Less booze. I guess I deserved it. I wish I had taken more photographs of the prairie, back when I lived there, when a bronzy skyline still existed. When the tornados came, the old lady with the crystals called it a twirlwind. She was so pretty, muttering that word, I could've kissed her tissue cheeks, I could've gathered up every shattered piece of her crockery. Now my brother helps her keep chickens, I picture him lugging big bags of feed across sienna plains. I don't remember the old lady's name.

I like the word twirlwind, its innocence.

I like the things that I like, but I love everything. Sometimes that hurts. And hurts and hurts. And then stops or even ceases to be.

My brother texting *why don't you visit me?*

The bars of a phone battery slowly depleting. It seems they run out quicker with each new model. I wish I were allergic to electricity, like that guy from *Better Call Saul*, the brother whose house is on lockdown, covered wall to wall in silver foil. Allergy became an addiction for him. His fortress a pharmakon. I could hone another version, snapping cetirizine in two and missing you. Without electricity, would I still covet your messages?

In our current era, I'd say we operate on the level of amorphous communication. You are the flash of yellow in a Per Kirkeby painting, who died the other day, or maybe the yellow is me. Is in me. There was one of his paintings in the gallery, accented with markings in yellow. I was starting to forget where yellow came from, projecting its scent on the floor tiles. Being in the gallery for too long made my head swim. In all that yellow, I craved the cool illusions of indigo. Yellow, colour of pus and sun, was too real altogether. Yellow was illness. The jealous light of Ada. Failing spells. Smoker's teeth.

The dirty landscapes all looked the same, clouds curdling around lukewarm mountains. I did not like how they made me think of my body. Undulant, arid structures.

I miss greener valleys.

The south side is aflush with tree-lined streets. I'm not saying it's simply the suburbs. We have ferns here, lush quantities of temporary blossom. I can hardly walk on my knee, but the pink and the white and the green just kill me. Grossly I admit, you were my favourite ephemerality. I love the word avenue forever.

There were notes I don't recall making. A neo-gothic edifice, a purely aesthetic childhood. Ada, a name meaning 'ornament' in Hebrew.

Her wild hands. Deadly nightshade.

Liv's favourite record is Lana Del Rey's *Ultraviolence*. It's Lana's New York record, monochrome and oozing with hipsterisms and party aftermaths; so much so that her voice emits the steam off the streets. It feels dirty with the neverend of summer. She positively glistens with longing but then collapses all that pull through insouciant cool. The openness of those songs, arena-ready, too languorous for parties. I remember Liv had that album on vinyl; she loved the warmth of the crackle and drag of Dan Auerbach guitars. I listened to it over and over, trying to understand the parts of Liv's life I could not otherwise. She said she needed LDR to wind down, a cure for all mania. She confected of her anxiety a rich hyperbole. *Ultraviolence* was Kate Braverman cross-processed then reduced to monochrome, a minor key, a greyscale. We were on the wrong side of America. Being heroines: rock bottom, blackness and blue of relief. A blackness that was never quite black, not fully void but a sort of luxuriant analogue halftone. Those songs saved us. I thought of scorched-out palms, glitching on the tide lines of Los Angeles. That would come later. Someone adding a fade effect to their picture. The residue sway. For now we were coastless. We sat up in some bedroom on the top floor, watching the street below, smoking out the window. You said you used to do this after every shift, come home at four in the morning, smoke out the window. Roll your own. 'Cruel World' did something shimmery to your organs. You seemed to draw a deeper bliss from it than Liv did, which is saying something. Lana as masculinity's analgesia. Liv, I think she just liked the sorrow. That was okay also, all of us inclined to sorrow and imaginary skylines.

There was the year Liv did nothing but smoke weed all day, waiting tables at a restaurant downtown that sold fresh hummus and heaps of oven-baked pitta. The occasional salad leaf that locals called Rucola. Nobody in that restaurant willingly spoke English; tourists were shunned. Liv loved it. She learned German in weeks, catching vowels on her tongue, consonant trigonometry. When I stayed over in spring, she made us go out wearing matching red dresses, drinking creme de menthe at some festival in Tiergarten. I think Liv knew how the red dress, complemented by creme de menthe, brought out her emerald eyes. She borrowed this from a book for young adults, written a hundred years ago. Her instinct for colour: one of the many reasons she got rich. I tried not to be jealous. I had déjà vu just for her. She found this whole life. I knew this was the fate of our sisterhood just like the fictional, coming-of-age consciousness I'd loved as a child. She took long, hot, indulgent baths. Back home, I listened to *Ultraviolence* while brushing the smoke out my hair on Sunday. 'The Other Woman,' last track on that album, was like glass in my throat being smoothed and softened. The voice of a mistress. Sea, the sea. It's the way you wake up in his eyes when he comes; when you don't know if he is here or there, with you or her. But then that quick glimmer worth every uncertainty. We'll brush fingertips in a club somewhere, someday; or maybe I won't see you again. Maybe I'll see you in someone else's eyes but know it's you really. When he apologies for coming inside you, like once there was a key and the lock, who cares. The other woman will never have his love to keep quiet. Her sultry heartbreak, that gorgeous lift of her voice above languid, ironic sax. The pictures of cats in other countries, black and white ones all over your Instagram. Even the b-sides were amazing, tales of lilac pills and Hollywood hills, lonely dealers and dangerous beauties. I started to understand what Liv loved about this record. The razored parts of romance, its serrated remainders, the fissures between us. The possibility of a love you'd cut your capillaries for, wear white denim and watch smog-ridden sunsets alone from the top of a stranger's apartment building, ten years older. Relish the bleed in secrets. Berlin was full of hidden places. I guess a lot like New York. What did I really know of either. It was just so huge. There was something slow and jazzy about this record, like Lana had swallowed her bluets, Schuyler-eyed, unnatural-strength brandy, her voice accented with silvers and greys like threads of starlight. The record just before she learned how to vape. Then the air would plume into candy. For now, the quality of swing, ornaments of breathy harmony. I hide in these concrete cocoons, just listening.

Liv was dismissive of magic, but she used to say, sincerely, "This album is spellbinding." She'd light her spliff by the pool and I'd watch its small glow dance in the air above our indigo.

Remember that time you met Liv, for real. When you came to Berlin, like a miracle. I remember you at the airport, how you'd lost your bags but you didn't care, you were just happy to see me. How you said I smelled good; you were drunk on bloody marys from the plane. When we said goodbye a week later, you admitted, "I like Liv a lot, she's so bonnie."

I cried in the mirror that night, because we were out of each other's zones again; there was that photo I'd taken of your wrist, petting the wee stray kitten in Liv's garden. The way your veins rose, true and green. How strong they looked, clasped in a single bracelet of ochres and orange. I cried because I could hardly imagine being held again by anyone. My tears were luxurious and strange, so intermittent they felt chandeliereal. They belonged to a girl who coveted her sorrow. I was no longer allowed to be her. I had to disavow all that.

My guardian angel updates her Facebook: Oh to be a cat sunning in tangerine county. She posts holiday photos, checks in her location with dream coordinates. It's as though she were there now, a distant present. Maybe we leave pieces of ourselves wherever we go. Maybe we want someone to find them, nourish them. Maybe love is just extinction's proximity to sunlight. Maybe you are supposed to put it all back together.

Where did we really start?

For a week I ate nothing but strings of bright green celery, snapped between my teeth intermittently. I felt so frail, it was like falling into your arms again. I'd fall over and over. I'd lose the words to claw back with, scratching the full stops like fragments of pepper.

When it happened, all I could muster were heart emojis. Here we are, too soon, too soon <3 <3.

I'm sorry I lacked the eloquence then, always operating at less than 80%. Soon, I lost the sense of here at all. Liv kept sending me YouTube videos of her favourite songs slowed down by 800%. I would listen for about 30 seconds until the nausea set in.

What's the name of that condition musicians get, where after ten years their muscles are so wearied that often they'll twitch without warning. Curse of the violinist's precision. A mark that the body's limits are shivering, as if too many times you've exhausted every repetitive regime of motion. But how sweet the melody when perfected.

People back home used to say, when I described the pool in Berlin to them, Aren't you just fetishising this whole Hockney thing with a Kreuzberg twist? Isn't that so fucking corny? I thought of what they meant, the turquoise and the flat colour and the splash. Artworks of a lover's t-shirt. Tried to categorise divisions of irony and sincerity. Thinning down what was there all along. An architecture of rare terracotta. I said it wasn't that at all. If anything, the pool was something from *The Secret Garden*, this hidden realm of serenity, this innocence. There was nothing suburban about it really. I could be naked here. Nothing so geometric, so clean. You'd find the garden, Liv's leaf-ridden yard, at the back of a wardrobe, pushing back knitwear like foliage. The overgrown element, the excessive gold finish of the ladder; anachronous maybe, a glitch in forever.

I should've gone over.

*
**

Interesting fact about Lana: she was born on the summer solstice. She'll tell this to anyone who listens, which is 59,000,000 listeners a month. Something about the heat of that season, its breathless hinge of two halves of the year, Gemini into Cancer. Is this why she always sings of a longing for death? The rapture in climax then inevitable comedown, the slow-drawn dance towards solitude and autumn. Peeling away my greenness. In every press shot I've seen she is smoking so beautifully, raising her girls.

After it happened, when I should be feeling so wretched as to not leave the house, actually I walked for hours and saw beauty in the face of every stranger. That beauty felt wrong. It felt superimposed, an unsure source; but it was still so beautiful. I kind of just wanted to sit by a pool somewhere and watch people eat ice cream, passing with anonymous quantities of smiles and blow-dried hair and shaven legs. Everyone's eyes tucked behind dark glasses, souls that were cool and glassy as the eyes of cats. A lightness and smoothness. I didn't want to see eyes because they'd remind me of yours. The lost glister, feline flicker. Fuck the colours blue and green.

Is it possible to live unbounded and free? To live without the other in your blood like free-based adrenaline, having the flu for Christmas? To live coarse and singular as the flame-tipped grass of the prairie. To be clear again.

*
**

Liam, my old partner-in-crime at work, used to say I can't remember the last time I didn't wake up with a feeling of exhaustion and dread. Ah, ubiquitous dread. We hid it well. We were always pulling pranks on the universe. He enthused over other people's haircuts and we'd accidentally match our socks all the time, odd little colours like orange, sky blue or lilac. He often wore a baseball cap so when we spoke in clubs I was always banging my face off the visor, trying to get closer to the wise things he was saying, insights all blurred by thumping music.

Liam, Liam, Liam. We made a pact never to leave our terrible work, not unless something thrilling came up for both of us. Life put a rot in the heart I'd held pure for that.

He was always pursuing cute wee schemes, like pilfering money off customers for coffee instead of putting their orders through the till. I wanted to write a whole pamphlet of poems called *Millennial Revenge*, based on Liam's antics and their vision for a more just future.

Who else would I message, delirious in the morning unready for work?

Oh my god, sometimes I just wanted an adult sanity. To wake up clear-headed, and not in the fug of some terrible, invisible drug. Boredom was everywhere then. I bear it still.

A poem by Kevin Opstedal about a woman stripping her body to nude then bone then a pure white powder, something blown away in the wind. I craved it. My body at war with cellular miscellany.

The thing is, my favourite Lana record is her fourth, *Honeymoon*. It reminds me, maybe, of that ill-fated affair with Cam, and how you came later like afterglow. The prairie which sometimes resembled the ocean upside-down, the amber plains were sky and the blue-sky sea. The warm warm wind of the prairie. I thought of Hollywood, where I'd never been. The scorched-out palms which haunted me again, adjacent to the plaza of archetypes drinking cocktails of bourbon and blues in lieu of my hometown whisky. A haze of horizontal smog. Violaceous. To be that drunk and double. *Honeymoon* is the perfect synthesis of cerulean sorrow, freakish in parts but quietly sparkling, the slow-motion scenes in a David Lynch movie. Sometimes a claustrophobic production, deep trap beats apart from the anthemic outlook of previous records. Smoky vocals. Those grandiose and dark, cinematic strings. Billie Holiday, love in the wrong places, utterly self-sacrificial, roses between thighs, 24 hours, misunderstandings, a marijuana sunrise saved like a desktop. Every face a precarious rendering. Licks of guitar that fold into waves; 'Terrence Loves You' shimmering a clear, electric heat. *I lost myself.* Languid and fragile, to break upon endless delay. Baroque balladry. I remember that song came on in a basement supermarket in Mitte, and I cried and cried, pacing the vegetables then the packets of pills, painkilling, waiting for the end of that song, the thought of wherever you were, long gone.

It's not fashionable to dwell in sentimental music. The poppies in your mother's garden, bursting in the dark. I am lying upside down in the indigo pool, little bitch Gatsby. Whatever you wanna do, I'm here for it. Even in the future. I feel sick in myself.

Cam and I would pace the edgelands of the prairie, canoe up the creek at dusk when nobody else was around, not even the ranchers. Cam was so quiet, I would fill the silence with my chatter until it was more pleasant to just listen for the crickets, their blur of significant nowhere. Being with Cam was like finding yourself lost all over again. He smoked so much green I'd have to wash the smell out my hair each night before work. He smoked so much his eyes became twin red deserts. When we had sex, I mostly focused on the dilation of his pupils. That was my favourite part. The dissolving oil pulls of *Under the Skin*. I fantasised myself a legendary alien.

If he did talk, it was usually about this girl from his high school, Pippa Brownlee, who hit a deer with her motorbike. She didn't sound like a real person. We'd sit in the diner, listening to downbeat, creepy swing, our knees touching under the table. "And you know what she did," he'd say, over and over, "she just threw that goddamn carcass right into the creek!"

I remember Cam's 21st birthday, round at his grandmother's cottage, the taste of birthday cake, lavender icing like nothing I have tasted since. She treated me like her own tender something. She hesitated before everything she said. In this family words were rationed with the sort of extremity usually reserved for luxuries like chocolate or brandy. She scolded Cam for staring out of windows. Did she know where his mind was? Did the twist of my smile mean anything then?

I wanted more noise. It had to end.

*
**

Looking back, everything you said was sort of gilded. I'll save it for another year, you said. You said it so often, like you were building up this virtual future anterior, a personal city. I'd suggest things, ask if you were okay. I'll save it for another year. I love you; I save you for another year. I love you; I save for you another year. Like you were building an architecture of life to reassure me. This can't happen now, but we could speculate. There were our shadows, eating us alive.

Lostness, dawn. Tangential air of other accents. Ruthie read my tarot again, days before it happened. She watched me flipping the last card, the future card, but then grabbed my hand to stop me. Best to wait and see. How could she know? Did she?

Years later, I looked up Pippa Brownlee online. Her mugshot was all over Facebook, like that was a blue hilarity. Our only mutual friend was Ruthie, whose page hadn't been updated in forever anyway — I mean she still had plaits and freckles in her profile pic. Her name made me think of soft scuffed leather and gingham kitsch. I wonder what it was Pippa had done, long after her first crime, the killing of the deer. I remember we were at the diner and Cam pointed her out; the one time I saw her in real life. She was standing at the bar, sinking her teeth into the biggest chocolate cookie I'd ever seen, wiping the crumbs from her mouth with the back of her hand. There were so many holes in her tights, it made me think of the combs in a beehive. Trypophobia. There must've been so much sugar inside, eager to seep. When she spoke, passing by saying hi to Cam, ever so briefly, her voice crinkled all over like foil. It was kind of electric. I decided to add her.

Not long afterwards, the posts started coming in on her wall. RIP, sorry to hear, thinking of your family. Love you loads, prairie angel. A link to a news article. She died in a road accident, somewhere south of the prairie highway. I couldn't help picturing that luxury of milky brunette hair spilled out on the tarmac, splatters of blood, the lights going on and on around her. Clicking through the posts, I felt dizzy. Among the mourners I was looking for Cam's name. I did not find it. He wasn't exactly an enthusiast for textual expression.

I spoke to Ruthie and she said my aura had lightened from its original indigo. I wanted to kiss her, smack in the mouth.

"Stop it," she said, "you're high."

*
**

There were vines that grew outside your flat. In June they bloomed with clematis flowers. I pass by sometimes where the heads have withered, and the leaves look limp. Southside of town. I think about Lana's reading of T. S. Eliot's 'Burnt Norton,' track eight of *Honeymoon*. Time in time present, time's perpetual possibility, time as passage, time in the rose garden. I'm booking flights to Berlin again. Time in the honeycomb. I need to be in Liv's garden, sound of the honeybees, the religious quality of light on the pool. She'd fix us mint juleps like we were true bourgeois and I'd hug my knees by the water. There'd be pretzels laid out untouched on cheap china plates. I'd try not to shake with tears. I'd try to contain my salt, my water.

A limousine passed in the street, leaking lyrics: 'Lay Lady Lay.'

I remember that song, the first Dylan I'd heard, peeled from an acoustic compilation album my mother owned and which I soon burned onto a CD-R purloined from Asda. I remember being so excited by the idea of rolling fields through an open window, a car cruising the prairie; then this big white bed I could lay on, in the hazy fade of the afternoon. I'd do nothing; I'd imagine this big white bed, soft smooth linen like birthday cake icing where I'd lie and listen to the song till my skin creased like the sheets. I'd be alone but in my body half waiting to be scooped up, held then melted. That was my childish idea of lovemaking. Dreaming the crackle of vinyl in the hiss of insects on toast, I'd be in the grass and nobody would find me. The air tasted sweet as the honeydew, strawberry juice clotting. Why wait any longer for the world to begin? Did I realise then, preternaturally, that everything good in life is a sort of fling?

I remember hugging you goodbye on the swing, spinning round when you stood up, hugging so hard we nearly fell over. I remember walking home warm and elated and hungry for what I could not name.

Someone once said: when you lie to each other, over and over, that's love.

Listening to Sonic Youth's 'Drunken Butterfly.'

I thought of my body as a horrible canvas of porous holes.

Wtf.

I clutched my phone harder for how much I loved you.

You spent one summer in America and said time was different there.

My body full of holes, my salt tears leaking.

One time we were high, maybe a couple hours in and we'd done with cradling each other like children. The music had lulled to its usual grace. We sat some distance apart; an oasis among the chatter of others, carefully doling our words, worrying them like beads on a rosary. You were saying how you had this condition, a mutation of your father's. It was a metabolic thing, maybe thyroid-related, I don't remember. I should've remembered. The lore of your veins, the intensity. Sometimes you would black out; your blood pressure leapt or dropped. You avoided red meat and then meat altogether. You cut down on sugar and caffeine. I fainted in gigs and on airplanes. I ate everything. We walked all the way home in the bright July sunshine which was too much really for early evening, you were trembling, strange; you had to kneel on a kerb to catch your breath. I noticed then how the capillaries around your eyes had all burst, a perfect array of indigo, lilac. Your eyes were tiny flowers, around them corollas of pain. Are you okay? You made your way home alone from there and wouldn't let me go with you. You sent me a message to say thank you, avocado. Relief's sweet green.

I should've done better.

What could I have done?

I have never felt lust more than the lust of a thunderstorm. There are years now. There are gashes in the sky where the cloud comes out. I love the way it feels right before love cracks.

When you told me you'd been to America, the summer you spent there, I went and bought you one of my favourite Sufjan Stevens albums: *Greetings from Michigan: The Great Lake State*. You said you knew that song from *Little Miss Sunshine*. You said you'd listen. I'm not sure you ever did, but I used to fantasise about how I'd put the CD on in your room when you were in the shower or making food.

⁎⁎

I slept with someone else on the summer solstice. The absence of darkness that night. They pulled the plastic flower crown out of my hair and later I bled everywhere. I wished the day had ended; I was scared of how it just carried through. Everything stung in my life (and I would sting too).

What once was sweet and green, rolling our tongues like the leaf twists in marbles. We were too long for anyone.

Here I am, waiting on another train. All these hours I spent waiting up for a message, applying concealer thick on my neck.

Liv told me about this exhibition at the gallery. *Portraits of a Desert in Mourning*, it was called. Actually, Liv got it wrong in the message; I turned up and it was called *Portraits of a Desert in Morning*. I wasn't sure if the 'u' was added by accident or if she meant it. She said the photographs of the burned-out sand made her cry. For all the arachnids, the altered dunes, she said. I did not know what she meant by 'altered dunes.' All dunes look pretty much the same to me, although the deserts are different. I paid the €10 entrance fee and wandered around, shielding my eyes from the red light projected on each image with special gel cameras. Nothing was framed. There was a lot of double exposure, so you'd notice the correspondence between a line of sand and the undulations of land, the pinkish cirrus streaking the sky. If you looked for too long, the red light would form a haze on the surface of the image, so every shape melted into mirage. I found the pictures themselves, the subject matter, pretty trivial. I was more interested in the ghostlines around the exposure, the way maybe they portrayed a hidden landscape — one the viewer brought to the image. It was like at school, when the teacher knew I was bad at drawing so let me trace photographs from a lightbox. It was like brushing my pinkie over the contours of an Ordnance Survey map, finding the curves and twists in the grid. Making my spinal landscapes over, a doubling. The way something came clearer to life through fainter remnants, the paradox in that. The little ellipsis that rolled over and over, in the time it took you to type back to me.

All these read receipts, all these reasons.

In that era, I listened to Grouper's *Grid of Points* from start to finish each night until it gave me the bends — a nausea silver as her voice, streaming through the air as emotional tinsel. I imagined streams emitting from her throat and changing the flow of melody to mercury, connecting to lake time and epochal bedrooms. Chorales of static.

I kept skimming your messages.

The best parts, where my attention strayed from the lines. There retained a struggle.

From the gallery gift shop, I bought a postcard of the exhibition. The image had a slither of a moon in the background, but was otherwise just stretch marks of savannah, musky with crimson shrubbery, burnt skeletal by sun. It reminded me, I realised, of the prairie. Of Cam and Ruthie, afternoon blush and marijuana, cheap southern wine and lipstick. Mostly, though, just the endless sands, the eerie creek.

The way a prairie looks in the distance is like television static, the heat haze rising above it.

Cherry chapstick, cherry mentions,
cherry renditions. Cherry dye,

cherry blossom, cherry digits.
Losing cherry. Cherry picker.

Cherry infusion, cherry cola.
Cherry when you know it's over.

My friend tweeted something the other day, which made me smile. I sexually identify as sadness.

Because avoiding a bad appetitive love, because the necessity of
cigarette ideation and feminine pain.

*
**

Recently, quite out of character I bought a medium-sized coke and
sat in the window of the McDonalds in town. It was 4am and I
slurped a bright darkness, watching the dead street, kicking my
brogues against the glass. I didn't check to see if my paper cup
was recyclable. This was the last place on Earth to get a bona fide
plastic straw and I loved it. Everyone else in McDonalds was loud
and wrecked, but they did not sit. They were milling around, mock
dancing to the silence, stumbling. At the tables, there was just me
and a homeless man, who had emptied his day's change onto the
table before him and was spending a considerable amount of energy
shuffling those grubby pennies around. So there was the clink of
coins and the shouts of drunks, the dull thump of my shoes on the
glass. I kept thinking how all those coins meant memories, and
maybe the man was adding them up, click click click in precarious
towers. Then I felt dumb inventing that reason. Money is future-
oriented. Someone was squaring up to someone else. The coke
fizzed inside me and so I felt good, sugared, self-complete. The
deflation of course would come later. A family of weary-looking
tourists shoved in behind me; I saw their swollen silhouettes in the
window reflection. I saw a gaggle of glittery teenagers. I had to
google the word 'benediction.'

I did it again, last night. Sat in McDonalds; this time in another
country. Soaking in the absolute sense of nowhere. Deliberating a
purposeful sleeplessness. These streets are anonymous to me; their
names turn to wasps and ash in my mouth.

Sit for an hour, write a little. Ration my words. Soda. Ice crush, straw chew. Dolphins dying. Indigestible longing inside my stomach. Melted cheese.

*
* *

Back in your city, our city, I had a job interview. I walked around afterwards, still wearing the thigh-clinging pencil skirt and feeling as though my body were being gradually swallowed. I drank with a friend until she had to leave, conscious of work the next morning. Drank until dark, nursed another alone. Tennents for good measure, sweetly familiar tins with the silver, red and yellow. Passed by a club I used to frequent, but the name had changed. Posters in the window for bands whose names I didn't know. Crossed the street but looked back. There's Liam! Just standing outside the club, scrolling through his phone — same skinny jeans and cropped curls as ever. It's been years since I've seen him, especially with my recent media withdrawal. He's standing there, drinking a can of classic Coke as though it's the nineties. I can see the condensation upon that aluminium, the way the metallic red gleams against his mint green t-shirt. He looks like an advert. Time.

I wondered if he'd notice me.

Once, I would've jumped out at him to say hi; I would've grabbed his shoulders and spun him round. Nowadays, I'm scared of my body. The space between things. What counts as an aura, what the aura might do. I feel like I'm infecting the world with my indigo. I want to talk to him, though. I'm going to talk to him. But then a cab rolls by and Liam looks up from his phone, slides it into his back pocket, goes to step inside. I could've reached out, stepped across the street, waved frantically; I could've bloody messaged him later.

All these abstract narratives add up to something. The hours upon smudged hours. We talked about it once, we tried to get to the root of it, but everything was scrambled, ambiguous. Later you messaged about our failure, you said trying to understand was what, was like trying to masturbate on a comedown. I wondered what was personal and what was chemical.

Remember we finished working a bank holiday weekend and lay side by side in one of the restaurant booths, drinking purloined peach schnapps from the stockroom, replenishing all recent depletions of sanity and sugar? We were too tired even to change the music from the usual spooky lounge jazz, fell into its languid slumbers of piano and sax. We lay there, cracking jokes about the madness upstairs, the regulars.

Sometimes I'd wake in the middle of the night with a phrase of that music reeling round in my head.

Back then, someone was always offering to make you a cocktail. I'd sit at the bar after work and they'd keep on coming, draining my baggies of tips. Sometimes I sit in a dingy bar in town, waiting for Liv, too far north for the clutter of Kreuzberg, dreaming a thousand flambéed blood orange sunsets, cranberry and vodka splashed over ice and Cointreau.

When Liv does unexpected overtime, I walk all night and meet the dawn alone.

Berlin is so huge. It is many times the size of our city, this place I've moved back to. The comic book shop I pass on the way home has been closed for years and years, but they only started boarding it up a week ago. Remember you used to joke about its name, FUTURE SHOCK, and the fact that the shock of the future, for that shop, was that there was no future. As in, the mail accumulated on the floor, unopened, and such harrowing quantities of dust covered every surface. You could hardly see through the dusty windows, but certainly the shop had been empty for as long as any of us had lived there. There was always a 'U' missing in the sign, which read in big yellow letters: FUT RE SHOCK. Someone has taken down the cryptic, Comic Sans notice about picking up magazine subscriptions, the opening hours. They have taken down the yellow letters. I wonder what comes next, what constitutes a true extinction.

RE: SHOCK. FUCK.

The woman who printed my exhibition ticket at the gallery had the most extraordinary yellow talons. She caught me looking and smiled, "acrylics. Really nice place in town, cheap too." She looked pleased with herself, as if she'd just handed me a gift I didn't deserve. The nails reminded me of the goldenrod that used to grow down the creek, exploding with ochre against the darker reeds. I loved to brush my fingers through it, fondling the yellow like a piece of chamois clothing; something crumbly then soft and leathery, wanted.

That time I went walking with Ruthie and she picked a thick blade of grass and showed me how to whistle with it, but I couldn't perfect the necessary vibrations.

There were other botanicals, of course: swamp flowers that grew out of murky waters. Mostly you just noticed their noxious pungency. Cam didn't care for names but knew them anyway, would mention to me in his throwaway air, like Marlene I can't come out today, Dad needs me to cut back the milkweed. Swampy or showy? Milkweed, he said, made the animals vomit to chew on. It smelled of cinnamon. I used to wonder what bit you were supposed to eat to make yourself sick. This was later, after I met you. I used to worry I wasn't thin enough for you — not that you ever mentioned it, or maybe even noticed my body at all. Your arms were so perfectly sculpted; how could you ever think about the imperfections of others? If I had arms like yours, I'd admire them all day. I'd stretch them in front of me, watching the muscles glimmer and twitch beneath the tattoos, which twisted and clicked when you raised your arms. I can't talk about your tattoos, not really — that would identify you too strongly.

Sometimes when I write it is like taking my clothes off in front of uncertain company. Making myself into a big nude no one. The first time I got out my breasts on a webcam, I felt as though the screen's electricity had transferred to my arteries. My face gleamed for days like cathode radiance forever in me. I was powerful. My cells were multiplying strangely. I had not needed to write; I just presented myself. My veins raised indigo, lit by a screen.

Type back to me, please. Type good and slowly. Picture the endless strip tease of the city, its trees still skirting our nacreous streets.

Nothing much else in life works quite like that, at least as easy. In the temporary.

We saw something in the creek, Cam and I. Saw in the turbid water what wasn't a beaver or one of the jackrabbits that occasionally skirted our vision. There was a heap of waterlogged clothes and the lumpen shadows of something beneath the surface, a shape well-hidden by the reeds. Cam clutched my arm — we were walking along the edge of the creek, legs skimming the long grasses. He hissed at me to turn back. I was so scared I just did as I was told. I walked back to his father's fishing hut and waited, drawing circles in the dust with my fingers and eating stale ginger biscuits, shaking. I was too scared to turn on the television: the sound of the generator would startle the birds that gathered at the window. I watched the birds awhile, sparrows the colour of chestnut mushrooms. Cam was gone a long time, an hour or more. He came back red-eyed.

"You didn't see anything, did you?" he said. I shook my head. We were so young then.

A few weeks after this incident, we discovered his father's stash of porno tapes, hidden behind the stacks of maps and rods he kept in the fishing hut. Cam's father would go away for weeks at a time, to help on farms. He called himself, wryly, a 'freelance peasant labourer,' sank glass after glass of Jack Daniels at mealtimes, sans ice. Cam said they only ever had mealtimes when I was around. So I kept coming. I brought little cakes my mother made, slipped packets of cigarettes up my sleeve from corner shop counters. Cam said smoking cleared the air from his lungs. The smouldering embers of his cigarettes joined the flame glow of the prairie at dusk. And when he turned on his phone, the red light from the power would glow too. And when he pressed himself against me, my body became red and I knew the whole prairie could see it, the glow within me, red of my flesh. Sometimes you'd see clusters of fireflies in the distance.

We spent a whole afternoon, watching those tapes on his father's VCR. It got pretty hairy. I maintained an expression of polite disinterest throughout; I wanted to look away but could not. Cam was staring so intently. Occasionally he'd reach over the space between us and grip my thigh, which was bare and pockmarked with midge bites in that healthy teenage way, my blood too sweet. He'd squeeze my flesh so hard there'd be bruises afterwards. His breath would draw sharp then release. He didn't do anything else, just that. He didn't reach further. The catch and release. Maybe seven times in the four hours we spent in that hut, watching those movies. I remember thinking of every scene: *hurry up already*. It wasn't quite dark by the time we ran out of stuff to watch. I told him I had to go, but that only seemed to make him want me – or something beyond me – more. My eyes were shining.

None of this is melodrama. I wouldn't want that at all; it was different with you.

When you said, "I don't want that to happen again, we need to be careful," I thought everything was extremely scary. But I did another line and murmured coldly, "no, no, of course not — no drama."

We were always full of lines like that, at the time.

It was so cold, that November, but then I grew warm. It all spread through me, sparkling, and I knew this was it. Serotonin seeping. Loving you was its own addiction, distinct from the powder we snorted and dabbed but did not need, not really. Or maybe you did and I didn't. Still, we always split our lines in two. We sat up through dawn with our music, only sometimes speaking, harsh with January. The final outside.

I find myself divided in a state of elation.

Shaking the ink from my pen. In that video, the one for 'Easy /
Lucky / Free,' Conor Oberst writes on glass about reality. When
he writes heaven, there's a line down bleeding. The screams are
muted by the onward beat, the guitar sounds like an exhalation,
post-attempt. Each note glides. You'd breathe in your still white
sheets; you'd open your eyes to the ceiling. I used to dream about
that. I wanted it so bad. The hospital walls were teal green, like
the door in that video. Do you remember that? There is nothing,
nothing, nothing…

*
**

Ruthie told me it would help to write down affirmations. They don't
have to be elaborate, she said, but simple and focused.

I feel like I am twelve again, scribbling pop punk lyrics at the back of
my school jotter. I avoid going home because every street is haunted.
I sit in Liv's garden, writing the affirmations; I'll sit there for as long
as she lets me; for as long as the weather stays warm in Berlin. There
is a limit to everything.

   Silence: It is not okay to say I would rather be sleeping.

   Geology: The earth will go on without me, which is a relief.

   Rising: I will sleep through the night and awake refreshed.

   Germany: Every airport is the intersection between here and
   there and home. An airport remembers where you came from.
   There is no way to avoid this.

   Rain: When it cools on the prairie I'm small again.

<u>Diurnal</u>: There is no way to escape your lostness. I can't find you again. I shouldn't even try.

<u>Willow</u>: It is good to smile sometimes.

<u>Promise</u>: Kill about half of your darlings.

<u>Logic:</u> Merely to write refreshes me.

I type up the words and send them by email to Ruthie. She replies saying "stop being so poetic, put your whole pussy into it." She attaches a recommended affirmations template, the one distributed on her counselling course. She says try this. I do not reply.

Perhaps moving to a city, so as to move through another, was an act of automatic elegy.

I would go out at night, just to look for life.

Like once there was this kid riding round on his scooter. It looked like he was twirling on a gauze of water; red and green, reflected in the closed museum. I thought in binaural beats of meditation tapes, and the mildness of being 25 and wanting to be properly cold and wearing all these layers and feeling sorry for myself, overfull and sick; a houseful of sick things; my mother crying, bits of toilet paper stuck to her eyelids from crying without tissues; the latticing sensation of dailiness, wanting someone to pull me taut as a bodice, splayed arms, sick and unsure; wanting to jump out of windows into swimming pools; wanting to curl my hair, wanting to straighten your heart. That kid will grow up for what?

Tomorrow very drunk I'll get good at myself.

I love the word savannah. Its soft vibration that briefly passes the lips, a sense slightly biblical.

It's difficult to admit that maybe I miss the prairie as much as I miss you. The older I get, the more its pixels slip away. I'm less morbid than I was, but even that feels like a betrayal. Scraping my way out of sadness. I keep thinking you'll message me, in the dead of night like you used to. I keep thinking, is that possible.

You said when I spoke, I was usually rambling. You understood maybe half of what I said. You were being facetious, slanting the truth. It was easier if I wrote to you, wrote you. I'd give up all my vocabulary, clean for that. Write into you. The nostalgic twentieth century fadeouts. How many all-nights spent watching these videos, making our time two-dimensional?

At the performance my friend, dressed as a Brutalist building, bellowed:

Who likes meaning?
Marlene has a very complex relationship to meaning.

Imagine this was one great letter, written especially for you. Liv thinks I am doing work but I am typing, typing slowly to you — choosing my words carefully, like fruit.

I fear I am missing something. Clicking for vitamins.

The smell of hot coffee is infinite comfort. I'm reminded of mornings in my old job when I had less to think about. When I had all the free time to think about you, playing over those fantasies. Another sting. I kept revisiting, masochistically, a hive of bees. The coupling and sticky uncoupling. The fucked up, remnant honey.

My fingers were red and swollen. Now they crumple, sore, and the whorls are emphatic. I am no longer no one.

Cam was so serious in bed, always full of intent, flipping positions and grunting. I wanted to come up for air and run.

*
**

A new habit of looking up crystal specimens on eBay. I imagine a forest of gemstones clustering the computer at my office desk, sucking up that techno-energy. I try to send more interesting emails. I buy nothing. I send Ada the most unwholesome memes.

An indigo child, according to gaia.com, is 'an upgraded blueprint of humanity,' 'gifted souls, on a clear mission to challenge and shift reality.' They are special and they know it, perceptive and enriched with high expectations of themselves and others. Often unable to delineate singular purpose from life. Often frustrated and prone to depression. The indigo blues. You always made strange observations, asked peculiar questions. We were each of a weirdness.

An old soul. Indigo boy and cherry girl. I dyed my hair redder when you left. I thought of my dad who messed around with who, her and god.

Sometimes it's like, won't you just come over now and cry in the shower with me? I don't ask for much. Your sadness is a mystery to me; let me get into it, sparkling, the last refreshment; you don't have to ask.

My hair washes out streaks of red in the water. It is more like strains of fruit than blood. The red is necessary.

Every time I visit Ruthie I pray she will tell me my aura is indigo still. It keeps happening, until one day she remarks with some interest, *You're very cobalt today, very bright blue indeed.* The news is overwhelming. I wonder if she is playing tricks with me, realising I am entirely at her perceptive mercy. I do not cry when she gets back on a plane. I look through her eyes, looking out at the blue. In fact, it is overcast for weeks. She's just added Walden, Amaro or Juno.

I felt best nude in the hours without you, just afterwards. You said you would end things but in the end you would fix them, patch them up with new words I never heard because what you told me in the night was always different. I walked in the streets as they filled with Maytide and everything was perfume and blooming. It felt as though every stranger passing could see right through to the flesh — how strange it was yours. Nothing is over. Our patchwork narrative would survive even that.

I keep going away but here I am. The nude body so white, like wax. The nude body still marked with rivulets of you. Bumps where I shaved. I try not to dwell on or trace the wounded code of them. I am very bad at staying away from myself. Avoiding the nude. Ruthie is back home, sending me photographs of the prairie which I cannot open, they are strangely encrypted. She says she read the milkman's tarot. She said there was an alarming quantity of swords. I wonder if maybe she wasn't supposed to tell me.

It's a very real worry that one day someone will hack and delete all our messages.

I miss the prairie tan of my teenage daze.

Here again the question, Are you still single? I answer it with the admission of a woman in jail, as though my solitary confinement was imposed. I suppose it was. Is love an imposition? I run out of things to say to acquaintances, who always look for an opening.

I walk home through the sinuous park trails where I'm not supposed to go after dark, looking again for a moonbow. Voicemails from Ruthie on my phone, asking again about the affirmations. "Well did you?"

There was a conversation I had with a waiter at work. I went back in on my visit to see him and whoever else remained — not many. He brought me coffee and told me a story about how recently he had visited Glencoe and was on the shores of some loch when he noticed a tiny island, maybe thirty-odd metres out from the land. He and his girlfriend, who was over from Canada, were sitting there awhile when they suddenly realised there were deer on the tiny island. Maybe three or four deer, whose silhouettes they made out against the silver water. We were like, how in the hell did deer get onto an island — did they swim? I was curious, I drank my coffee and listened. The coffee tasted of so many stressful mornings at work; it was awfully bitter, burned, but I loved it. My tongue excoriated on comfort.

"What happened next was we saw one of the deer get into the water and actually swim towards the shore. It was amazing. I've never seen anything like it."

I had no idea deer could swim either. We shared this image in the silent restaurant, a single deer swimming towards us. The grace in that, the strangeness.

Deer are such antique animals.

That time I wore my new patent shoes to work and you remarked, "They're shinier than my future." I could not help a wry smile as I said same. The shoes pinched and burned my feet all shift, so I got the fear about wearing them later. Every movement had burned in those hours, burned right clean through my flesh.

In a way, you already knew what would happen. Perhaps. I do laps of Liv's pool, as if each repeat is a backwards passage; if I swim enough laps I'll get back to you. The plash of the water a cool phraseology, that vague and musical familiarity.

We both used to talk about wanting to learn the piano. I imagined our talent as a kind of hologram refracting. I wanted to be whole together, but we came into parts: we shimmered different. I would skip youth into bass for you. I would learn the long and the slow notes, learn again your name, play the rhythm I could only make with you.

Without context, you once texted me saying: "My mother just called me lachrymose. Can you explain what the hell that means to me?" I tried to phone you, but you did not pick up. At the end of the text was a droplet emoji, watery blue. I wanted to know what had happened. How little I really knew you.

The awkwardness at work when we talk about weather.

I try to face the day. She is made of pasteurised light. In the mirror, I make myself up with shrapnel of eyeliner. I become darkening.

You know, you could tell me where you are. Any time. It's like, sometimes I think you might still ask me out.

My eyes glow red from chlorine.

I miss the keyboard of your wit, its openness.

I'm here, for now. My bright blue aura, the indigo water. Exquisitely less.

I curl into spaces where nobody sees me. I choose the top bunk in hostels, or swim to the bottom of the pool, touching the grate where the leaves get stuck in autumn. My body continues to bleed by the moon, so painfully exactly. Walking the city streets, I find myself cooing after strays with sympathy.

I did not grow up with cats but there was always Ruthie's. The old thing must be well into its ageing teens, whatever that is in cat years. She was a rescue and thus indestructible. Cleo used to prowl around Ruthie's garden, a yard of wildflowers that backed onto the prairie. She'd disappear for weeks at a time then come back angry, feral, almost deranged. She'd attack birds with extraordinarily brutal methods. She'd bring back dormice, baby rabbits and other mammals, her jaw dripping with blood the colour of the sun at dusk, her fur thickened gold by prairie dust. She'd leave her kill all around Ruthie's house. I remember Ruthie's mother used to weep in frustration; but they could not lock Cleo in or shut her out. Cleo would violate any order of space.

Ruthie bought a special spray online that would send her to sleep. She's got heart problems, Ruthie told me, during one instance in which I found myself the subject of Cleo's heterochromatic, wary stare. Anxiety, you could say. The spray smelled of aniseed and warm bodies. Ruthie said it released special cat pheromones, which reassured Cleo that she was at home. It was like duplicating the chemicals released whenever Cleo rubbed her tail around a table leg. I wondered if all that spray was having an effect on Ruthie, whether all those cat pheromones were upsetting her own chemical balance. I watched her for signs of feline potential. Would she start leaping from windows, or crawling under doors, purring and nuzzling the necks of men?

Many times since I have thought of that cat spray. In a coach, on a train or flight, watching the other passengers sleep: what I would give for one burst of soporific assurance that here, this can be home. A complete chemical change. The vapours that would salve my dislocation.

The tenderness in the sometimes stare of a stranger. When we share a sky.

Lilac wine, lilac wine. Nauseous every time. Then again connect; then missing my 5am friend, the absent presence. More bitter than you think.

*
**

No matter how long I stay here, I'll never tire of the strawberry stands across bluest Berlin. Blue because summer, blue because the otherwise grey is depleted. I could live off the fat red berries, the quality coffee from pop-up vendors. Each fleshy red heart, hidden inside. The juicy beat of the day, the bitten. I pace between stands, slowly erasing my afternoons. Work takes me nowhere, but I measure my steps.

    Tuesday: 28,439

    Wednesday: 14,034

    Saturday: 101

    Monday: 22,902

All over the city this summer there are posters for a band called Data Cartel. I turn corner after corner and again the same tropical graphics. Sometimes, printed in the tiny section of sky, above the text and the palms, I fancy I see a will-o'-the-wisp. Indigo splash upon blue. I extend my uncertain stay to attend the gig.

I returned to Liv's to find she was having her pool serviced. Properly, this time. No more insects or leaves or mysterious scents from the water. They would measure its pH levels and everything. It got me worried she was going to turn the place into an Airbnb. When I began complaining about it, she asked if I had been working lately. The question cut through me. Work is a dim, unremembered thing. The emails have gathered so long in my inbox, like the linden leaves on Liv's pool. It's like I was waiting for someone to come along and net away the stray debris. I have no idea how to compose a reply. She said, with stray irony, clipping mint leaves, don't let the freelance life fool you into idleness. Later, she poured me a coffee, strong off the stove. I opened the lid of my laptop. It seemed I had eons to catch up on.

Still thinking of you.

Later, we chilled at the lido, Liv's treat: €10 each. I wore a bikini and felt girlish, flicking the hair out my eyes. It was cooler than in town, a breeze off the river. I swam six laps and felt done with the world, in a pleasant way. It was good to just watch the sun go down behind the tall blue buildings, drinking bottles of beer laced with caffeine. My legs would bronze like the darkening sky and that fact of sensation felt adequate. I could forget you, even though you were the only one I wanted to see then, wanted you to look at my bronzing limbs and kiss the chlorine cool from my mouth.

From the little bar by the lido, you could watch boats go up and down the river. There were more boats than usual, that evening. I could have sworn I saw my name on the keel of one. I did not tell Liv about this. The name felt lucky, nomadic.

We did not go home to change. We went straight to a club and nobody even checked our IDs. I wore a lace top over my bikini, a denim mini skirt. Items we'd stuffed in bulging tote bags. There was so much dry ice in the room I could not see my own shoes, let alone the faces of those around me. Liv kept going up to men and biting their bottom lips, till they did something funny, pressing themselves against her stomach, hands on her butt. Then she'd shimmer away again. I did not look for expressions in the faces of men. I focused on feminine energy. I tried to dance to the techno, dance till my limbs were no longer mine. Liv always said I was bad at letting in strangers, which is true enough. She's someone who dwells forever in a state of osmosis, but I've got this shell. I started feeling light in the head, glimpsing the will-'o-the-wisp in the corner of the club. It would've been some glint, bounced off surface. Some glint, some glint of a strobe. I could have collapsed with tiredness. The music felt dirty. Diamantés shed copiously from the seams of my skirt.

Liv was strong from the factory; she was on her feet all day. She sank pints like a bloke. I danced and danced at her command; I did not catch anyone's eye. She said pretend they're all chlorophyll and you want them.

When I write in recline, I write more personally. This is me lying supine on a sofa that isn't mine, feeling vulnerable, hungover.

The tinnitus of the nightclub still ringing in my ear. I've been warned. There is this little white creature on my lap. German place names settled like boiled sweets at the back of my throat.

*
**

Would you believe it, walking home last night, we saw this stray kitten, snowy and fluffy against the ruthless asphalt. Skirting round a drain. I don't know the name of the street; the memory is hazy. My heart quivered, it shook for this tiny creature, as though it might fall down those nasty, rusted grates. I bundled the kitten among my lace top and carried it all the way home, Liv murmuring songs I didn't know in German. The kitten was quiet and sleeping. It did not wake until an hour ago and I kept checking through the night to make sure it was still alive. It looked like a creature from a whole other universe, far too white and clean to be wandering round here. It looked expensive.

I think the kitten came from behind the Mirror Fence.

"Maybe there will be a reward," Liv said, dressing for work.

I wasn't sure I'd ever be able to let the kitten go. I kissed its tiny pink ears and fed it saucers of water, watching the little pink tongue lap the clearness. My mother always told me it was black cats that were lucky, so I didn't hold any illusions about this one. Besides, there was still the matter of the will-o'-the-wisp. But anyway, she was clean and lovely and stayed awhile.

I kept her away from the indigo pool. We chilled inside and the kitten curled round my leg while I sent all my emails. There was a lot to catch up on. Every mew was a kiss through the ringing. I fell asleep like that, in the afternoon heat, black spots dancing before my eyes. When I woke up, the kitten was gone. The skin of my wrists pressed into my temples, a drop of Liv's bottled lavender.

I went out to look for the kitten, but all I could see was the newly cleaned pool, the salvias sprung up in the gravel of the neighbour's garden. An empty bottle of wine, a scattering of sparrows. If you didn't know, sparrows are the pigeons of Berlin. They are anxious for food, at once dirty and pretty. I searched the flat, shifted the furniture. Three times I checked the pool. I found myself crying in Liv's bedroom mirror, great fat girlish tears of loss. I was useless and shaking. The kitten left me, as everyone seemed to. I hadn't even had time to give her a name. When Liv came home, she held me tight on the bed and kissed my forehead and said, quite gently, it was probably time I went home. She said I needed to build a life again. She cooked me pasta but I could not swallow a thing, like every chew just hurt. Everything once more was slipping away.

That night I dreamed of the lava-like cirrus, moving gelatinous across the sky of the prairie. I felt homesick for somewhere I no longer wanted to be.

Instead of booking a flight, I went to see a piece of theatre conducted almost entirely through monitors, so that the limbs of the actors were shown apart from their faces. In that whir of synecdoche, I thought of the separate wants of my body. The play was about lust in the time of apocalypse, or something of that ilk. It was all in German, so I couldn't really tell. German words often sound like rumbles of thunder. There's a lowing in my belly and I want to get out of the theatre and shriek in the street. I want the rain to come, the sky to break. One of the actresses steps out of her screen. She unravels her long Ophelia hair and all the static rises behind her as currents of water in streams. People in the front row of the audience start pelting her with artificial flowers. She begins soliloquising in her version of German. She feigns death, I suppose, among the piles of plastic flowers. I wonder if the audience members at the front are all actors, co-stars, plants. How many among us. The screens go black before the curtain drops. I swallow something jagged and impossible, like a mutant peanut. I couldn't help but think about Cam, squeezing my thigh in the dark. I spill white wine on my shoes and in the atrium outside, talk to no one.

I wile away days in the gallery again. Liv is getting restless with my presence, I can tell.

She grows sick of my moping around, my tangled laptop cord like a snake in the centre of her carpet. I start trying to cook her dinners, ready for when she's home from work, but she takes pity on my limp nests of noodles and we order takeout almost every night. It's not that you overdo the salt, she says. I want a recipe that sticks exactly.

It's maybe just easier to cook in your head.

She doesn't need to know about the state of the home I'll return to.

I take her to the gig because I don't want to go alone and I hardly know anyone in this city, gorgeous and splintering and blue as it is. Liv talks with a subtle German accent now, even in English. She pauses before replying.

"What is this 'Data Cartel?'"

The gig is filling up fast in the bounds of Treptower Park. My ankles brush the long grass as we try to find a spot. Some DJ blasts psytrance from the stage and rush of claustrophobia hits me, the hot bright muscle of my heart. I want to sit down in the verge by the trees but Liv leads me closer to the front. Liv thinks they are my favourite band; she's come for the occasion of my happiness. I merely peeled their name from a poster.

Liv was picking salad leaves out of her teeth, using the front camera of her phone as a mirror.

Data Cartel were wasted. Barely got their lips and instruments near the mic, staggering around, running hands through hair and sweat.

I was growing weak from all the standing. There was a darkening pressure in the air; I could feel it rise behind the bones of my chest. Growls of distant thunder and fat, low-hanging cloud the colour of industrial smoke. The band were singing about unrequited love now, some measure of self-sacrificial lyrics. Screams of girls. I wanted all this to be political: the discharge of wasted desire in the air. Nobody else seemed to notice the thunder; it was so low and hardly audible above the thrumming bass. The singer was ageless with bleached hair and sunglasses.

Suddenly, flashes of lightning blistered the sky beyond the stage. There was no horizon of course – we were surrounded by trees – but still the white-gold crackled the sky like foil. There was an urge, a fire in me. I wanted the trees to catch flames; I lusted for collective perishing. I felt dizzy off the thought. People were still screaming with joy at the music. With all the stage lights, how could the band notice the lightning? It seemed entirely possible that a tree or two would spark and then the whole stage would blow up. It was glorious, to feel this legitimately histrionic.

"We should leave, definitely," Liv hissed in my ear. She has an anxious sense for weather. She can't handle the extremity. I told her to go on ahead without me; told her I'd be straight home when they stopped playing. I tried to make a convincing performance of enjoying the gig and she believed me, popping aspirin on her tongue, shrugging, then pushing her way out the crowd.

"You have your own keys." More thunder.

The sky eventually cracked, gave way to rain. It was rain from another time, making everything a glistering delirium. The air still so hot. The set not finished. The singer was coming to a sort of climax, howling into the microphone as though he'd done imbuing it with the audio pleasure of all his pain. I loved him for his pain, his fuckable irony. It seemed unreachable and expensive, thus delicious. I swilled the last of my cider. Steam was rising around me. The rain came over my whole body, soaked my clothes and rucksack. People were starting to dash away. Only the high and obsessed remained in the centre. When the gig finally finished, I ran all the way home, startled with laughter. I stopped at various places, hiding under doorways. I caught my breath in shadows and tapped cigarettes from strangers. They wanted to talk about the set. I took shelter in the way they spoke to each other. I could be a bystander to the ease of their smoking and kissing. I told them my name was Lena.

*
**

The same kinds of gothic exception. Places I wanted to hide. The city was full of secret gardens and so many reasons not to go home. Briefly harboured the desire to wake up on a bench at six in the morning, surrounded by ravenous sparrows. The crazy old women would throw bread at me, as though I had ventured foolishly onto their territory. Three missed calls from Liv. I brushed my fingers against the cool bright stone of a warehouse, adjacent to a plot of soldered land that was once a park, ghost-grass replaced by trampled clay. Water was spilling off my fringe and onto my lips, my clothes stuck through to my skin. Somewhere not far off there were sirens. I guess I was shivering. I leant against the empty fountain, centring the desolate square, promptly vomited into its concrete bowels. It swirled among the fizzy remainders of my carbonated sick and I thought of a word my brother used once, in this cafe when they served him his milky coffee: *synergy*. Something you'd scrawl on a flip chart, make some extravagant gesture with your arms. Sirens again. Rain. Ring of aeolian phone.

The city with stipplings of tree-lined avenues, each shimmer of leaf-like suspended confetti. The way the sun moves west and drags with it the green, the green that needs gold. I would need to leave.

The pennies in the winterized fountain turn prematurely ferric with weather, turn from gold to green. Leaves fall along with our wishes.

When you were here, things were more still, they were perfect. I
knew them.

***
****

Fresh from a heath and sipping cherry coke from a grocer in some
faraway village, I am a protagonist. Out of sorts. The air-conditioned
airport, the way my lungs feel jealous of anywhere. Sucked into the
deep mordacious blue. I've only ever had three true flying dreams;
my problem is a lack of faith in systems. I'm suspicious that each
setup, the run-through and process, is haunted with an ulterior
logic. One that stems from a carefully placed bug, a set of fatal
conditionals. I dwell at the coffee kiosk for long enough that the
barista strikes a conversation. Their lovely accent I will miss, the
curious jolting music of it thrusting against English. I ask if they
have cherry-flavoured cola and they shake their head, bemused.
With one more stamp I could get a drink for free, but I don't have
time. I bite the apple into language and I do it over and over until it
is gone and yesterday.

I was always falling asleep on planes, the air sucked clean from
my lungs by a whirring, delirious throb. Thorns in my ears, a
burgeoning pressure I swore would draw blood.

Delays again. I take a ballpoint pen from my bag, draw from its
inky rattle the familiar lines on my wrist. I am getting better at this.
Ignoring the screens, the secrets.

***
****

You know it was Liam who designed my tattoo; I mean the one I
never got in the end, the one I still trace by memory. The original

sketch is clamped in a book of so and so's selected poems, which I accidentally gave to charity when I was leaving to spend time in Germany. Someone else out there might have it now. Precious sketch of the pool, which Liam reimagined from a painting by Henri Matisse, *La piscine*. It was not in Liam's usual style, its typical crispness of symmetry and lines; the blueprint tattoo was more fluid. He'd never seen Liv's pool of course, hardly understood why I wanted to carry it around with any permanence. But he trusted my vision.

"It's like the aftermath of our fast-food nocturnes," I offered. "The cool serenity."

He would not look at the photograph I showed him. He said he'd rather dream it with me.

I would've gotten that tattoo properly filled, with those fashionable watercolour inks of beautiful translucency. I would've paid a lot of money to get it done. I could've stomached any kind of pain for that image, but losing its sketch seemed significant, ominous. I'd let it elude me, so from then on I would only enjoy the pool as an outline of memory, mirage-like and slightly amazing. Fragile and vague. Splash of water, sense of those fallen leaves in October. The exquisite pain of first missing you. Tracing the borders that contained the water, the currents of remembrance I stirred with my limbs, my breath, my want.

Motivation, I once told you, is the colour peach. My least favourite, its feminine frenzy. After you'd laughed at me for using pastel-hued highlighters, instead of the office standards: yellow, orange, green and blue. We shared a tin of yellow peach slices, slippery and sweet on your friend's sofa where we were not supposed to be, four in the morning; you were flat-sitting and having problems and not wanting to go home. Grape juice alone still gets to me. A sunrise welcomed by halves, love bites, shoegaze. Metallic tongues.

Running substance, substance for running. Watched you turn away. Did all the watching scored to three. Eating peaches with you, line after line of colour tv.

Is this all of it, still dripping?

You said, "Sorry, Marlene." You said it while sleeping
              and I dreamed in our room again.

My love more than humanly possible
I thought to run out of words,
spiralling arousal.

Dive in the nerve pool.

Why?

ACKNOWLEDGEMENTS

Thank you to Kirsty Dunlop, Callie Gardner and Stuart Glen for reading earlier drafts of this manuscript, to Alice Brooker for editing and to Amy Grandvoinet and Poppy Cockburn for endorsements.

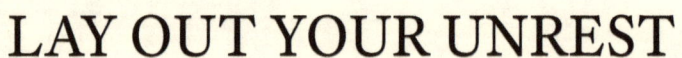

LAY OUT YOUR UNREST

www.ingramcontent.com/pod-product-compliance
Lightning Source LLC
Chambersburg PA
CBHW02080702726
47495CB00008B/2623